MISS HAWTHORNE SITS FOR A SPELL

MISS HAWTHORNE SITS FOR A SPELL

CHARITY SHOP HAUNTED MYSTERY BOOK THREE

KATHERINE HAYTON

Cover Design by kathay1973

ISBN-13: 978-0-9951007-5-6

CHAPTER ONE

Emily Curtis plonked the last box of antiques on the trestle table and stepped back to dust off her hands. Each time she made the trip to the local auction house, she could swear it took more effort than the last.

That's because you're getting old.

She snorted at the thought. Getting? She'd already gotten. With one day to go until her fifty-third birthday, it mightn't appear too large a number, but there were many times in the past year Emily hadn't thought she'd make it this far.

"Are you ready to tag the items?" a man called out from behind her.

Emily whirled around, seeing yet another new face. Since the first auctioneer's assistant had been let go of due to questionable accounting practices, every time she came here, the business had a new employee.

"I can't read or write, so hopefully you'll be able to help me out with that part."

A faint blush spread across her collarbone, a far cry from what the same admission would have produced just a few months ago. Every time Emily said the words aloud, they became easier to say.

"I'd be glad to," the man said, his ruddy cheeks and wide smile matching the enthusiasm in his voice. He tapped the nametag on his chest, "I'm Sean and I'm up for anything, so long as I get to sit down for a few minutes. They run us ragged, around here."

The three other patrons going about their business belied his words, but Emily smiled in gratitude. "Thanks so much. Do you mind if I look around in the meantime? There're a few more things on offer than I'm used to."

"Tell me about it." He dragged a chair up to the table and sat with a heavy sigh. "The storage unit place out on Belvedere Avenue sold off the overdue rental spaces in bulk lots. I think at least half of it's now come through here for resale."

Emily nodded though she hadn't even known Pinetar had storage spaces for rent. "Won't the folks who originally rented the spaces get upset if they see their possessions around town?"

"Probably." The man bent over the goods Emily had brought in for sale. "But they can hardly complain about losing something when they didn't pay for it. I talked to the owner a while back and he said he doesn't even consider it until the rent's gone past three months overdue."

Although the explanation was reasonable, Emily's heart broke a little as she began to search through the tagged goods ready for auction on Friday. When she searched for antiques among the boxes back at the charity shop, at least she knew the owners wanted them to go to a good cause.

Still, she wouldn't like to rent out space to someone and not be paid. To leave it so long was akin to stealing.

The first box searched, Emily moved on to the next. Another seller walked through the door, staggering under the load of two stacked crates. She kept him in her peripheral vision until he made it to the nearest table, then breathed a sigh of relief on his behalf.

A polished, stained piece of wood caught her eye and Emily tugged at a corner, thinking it might be a small picture frame. Instead, a chunky toy came free. Similar to a Rubik's cube in shape but with some cubes poking out further while others were sunken into the main.

"That's a puzzle," a voice said behind her and Emily turned to see Sean standing there, her itemised list in his hand. "I don't know if it's European or Asian or what but some of us have given it a go without success."

Emily held it out, turning it back and forth in the sunlight to make the stained colours glow. "How do you know if you've completed it?"

"The whole thing should open up, revealing a hidden design." Sean took it out of her hand and pressed against one of the protruding edges, smiling as it sank inward, only for another piece on the top to pop out. "I don't know what value it has in our twenty-four-hour entertainment world, but it's beautifully made."

He handed it back and Emily cradled it to her chest, possessiveness arriving out of nowhere. "Do the symbols on it mean anything?"

Sean shook his head. "Nah. Or, I should say, if they do, I'm not aware of it. We had an office girl check it out on the internet to see if it was a language or something. Turned out to be *or something.*"

She laughed and slid her forefinger into one of the recesses. The wood was so smooth it felt closer to marble, and the shine spoke of many layers of lacquer or varnish.

"How much is it worth?"

Sean's eyes narrowed, "Why? Are you thinking of bidding?"

"Maybe." Emily knew better than to show her actual level of interest. Despite the pang of loss it initiated, she replaced the puzzle into the box. "I've got a niece who likes that sort of thing."

The imaginary family member would be bitterly disappointed with the state of Emily's bank account. She pulled out another item from the same container, jumping as a jack sprang out of the metal tin.

"Ugh." Sean shuddered. "I can't stand the face painted on that thing. Please, put it away."

Although the sprung doll was a tad on the ugly side, it didn't impart the same sense of disgust in Emily, but she folded it away and clicked down the lid. "Is this from a toy maker or something?"

"Nothing so fancy," Sean said, reading the card on the table. "This is from one of those abandoned storage units." His frown deepened the longer he read. "Oh, that's sad. I remember this young woman, she used to work in the herbal dispensary. She was killed in a car accident late last year."

Emily's back jerked as though a shock of electricity had run through it. The blood drained from her face and a whine sounded deep inside her eardrum.

"Are you okay?"

"Just a dizzy spell." Emily held her hand up as Sean reached for her arm. "Just give me a second and I'll be fine."

He nodded and retreated a step, drumming his fingers on the table. "Can I call someone for you?"

"No, it's okay. I just get a bit lightheaded from time to time." When his face still showed concern, Emily lied, "My blood sugar sometimes drops a bit low."

Sean's face brightened. "There's a vending machine in the lobby. If you need a top-up, they have chocolate bars or dried fruit."

"Is that my sales list?" Emily said, nodding to the clipboard in his hand.

"Sure." He sprung the bulldog clip and handed the top sheet across to her. "I've got everything listed on there. It's a nice Wedgewood Dining Set."

Emily nodded and laughed. "It's great if you don't mind a few missing pieces."

"We get a lot of people through, hunting for one or two items to complete their set. I'm sure it'll fetch a good price."

"Well, the battered woman's shelter will appreciate it if it does." Emily couldn't resist turning to get a last look at the wooden puzzle box.

Sean followed her gaze and gave a small chuckle. "It'll be the third lot up for auction tomorrow if you want to come back then. If your niece is still interested, I doubt there'll be too much competition."

"Maybe." Emily chewed on her bottom lip for a second, creasing the fold of the paper in her hand. "Although, I don't have a lot of money to spare on presents, unfortunately."

"This economy will be the death of us all," Sean agreed with easy good humour. "But family's the strongest bond we'll ever have in our lives. Sometimes it's worth splurging, just to bring a smile to a loved one's face."

Emily thought of her only genuine family, a brother who had two years on her, very different from her invented niece. She wondered if he'd be more important to her if he'd had children—or she had, for that matter—then shook her head.

No use wondering when there were real tasks to get done.

She waved goodbye to Sean, who'd gone to help a new arrival, and forced herself to keep her eyes straight ahead, no matter how much they wanted to turn back and stare at the puzzle.

"YOU'RE BEING STUPID AND SENTIMENTAL," Emily whispered to herself as she sat and stared at the auction house door. "Better to turn around and get back to work, where you can do some good."

But she hadn't stopped thinking about the puzzle box from the moment she'd set eyes on it. It had caught onto her mind more firmly than any Chinese finger trap.

With a sigh, she gave in to the same urge that had carried her here and walked inside the hall. The neat rows of chairs laid out on the auction house floor only held a dozen people. Apart from a couple of men chatting down the back of the room, the place was deserted.

That boded well for her item.

Emily sat three rows back from the front, not wanting to appear too eager. She didn't bother to check in the box to see if she still wanted the puzzle. It tugged at her soul like a fish-hook, barbs holding it fast.

"Watch it," a young man called out as he pushed past the men at the back. The look of disgust he threw their way was only matched by the snarls they tossed back to him.

He shook his hair, the lanky strands audibly whipping through the air. A lattice of tattoos ran up the man's right arm, while the left had the silvery sheen of burn scars. Emily turned away as he glanced in her direction, not wanting to be caught staring. Not quick enough to escape a hazel-tinged glare.

"Our next item is a wooden puzzle box dating back to the turn of the century."

Emily sat up straighter in her seat, a faint frown creasing her forehead as she wondered how they could date the item when they couldn't even tell the country of origin. Not that it mattered to her. She just wanted to satisfy the urge in her fingertips to touch the smooth, wooden surface again.

The bidding started at one hundred dollars, startling Emily. Sure, the intricate details and frictionless movement of the piece lent it value, but she'd expected something less than half the price.

"One hundred," the tattooed young man said, holding his paddle up for good measure.

"One ten," she called back, a tremor of excitement making her hands shake.

"One twenty."

"One fifty." Emily lowered the paddle and swallowed hard, a trickle of sweat rolling down the side of her forehead. It was her top bid. To go there so quickly was a risk, but she didn't want to have the man lulled into the momentum of a gradual escalation.

"One seventy-five."

Emily blinked. She stared at the paddle in her hand, her teeth clenched together so hard her jaw ached. There was no way she could afford that, let alone top it. The supermarket wouldn't accept the excuse she needed a toy puzzle in lieu of payment.

"Sold."

The dizziness from the day before swept through Emily's head again, making her feel like it was spinning up towards the ceiling. The paddle clattered onto the floor as she gripped the edge of her chair, sweat bubbling up on her brow as she came close to fainting.

Get a grip. It's just a wooden puzzle. You can go into the Toy Warehouse and pick up something similar in balsa wood for five bucks!

No. Not something similar.

Emily had never seen anything as desirable.

CHAPTER TWO

When the rush of disappointment ebbed away, Emily stood and walked to the exit. Her foot caught on the floorboards, the rubber sole hitting at an angle so she tripped.

"Are you okay there?" a woman asked, jumping to her feet. She looked to be in her forties, only a decade below Emily's own age.

"I'm fine, thank you. All the excitement of auction just took me by surprise."

The woman's brow furrowed in confusion, and she stared around the almost-empty hall as though she'd missed something important. "Yeah, sure."

"I might just rest for a second," Emily said, taking a seat nearby. She didn't know why she was still talking to the woman. The stranger didn't really care.

Another few early morning patrons filed into the hall, taking seats wherever they fancied. Emily closed her eyes and tried to swallow back her disappointment. If she couldn't get control of herself, she wouldn't be able to trust herself to reach the car. She'd be stuck inside all day.

The remaining items in the lot were sold, one by one. As the next seller's goods were brought up to the main stand, the winners began a slow shuffle towards the cashier's desk.

"Wait," a voice cried out, sharp enough to split the air.

Emily turned, holding onto the seat back as she strained for a better view.

The cashier stood, her arm gripped tight onto the tattooed arm of the young man who'd won the bidding. "You can't put it on layaway." She pointed at the enormous sign that hung above her desk. "Rules of the auction, it's only a valid bid if you can pay."

As the man jerked away, another person stepped forward. Over six feet tall and with shoulders so broad Emily wondered that he could fit through a door, he appeared to be a security guard in the employ of the auction house.

The cashier stepped back and took her seat again, giving the enormous fellow a nod. She then turned to the next in line, a woman with her cash ready to hand over, her eyes wide at the unfolding scene.

With a lunge, Emily got to her feet and shuffled along the side of the hall as fast as she could go. That still meant the queue of payers had dissipated by the time she reached the back table.

"If he's not able to pay," she said, jerking her chin at the tattooed young man, "does that mean my bid wins and I can take the puzzle home?"

"Sod off," the man said, being rewarded with a shove forward from the security guard. "It's mine."

"It's only yours if you pay," the cashier said. "And unless things have altered in the last five minutes, you're not able to."

"I paid for everything else," he cried, waving his hand over a statue of other goods. "It's just one item I came up short for.

I told you, once I get to the bank, I'll have it sorted and make you whole."

"You don't have to do that, because we're not letting you leave with an item you can't pay for." The cashier shook her head, lips clamped into a thin line. "Honestly, I don't know why folks can't just read the conditions and abide by them. No cash, no bid. Simple as that."

Emily's head switched between the two of them like they were lobbing a ball back and forth. "But does that mean my bid now wins?"

"No," the young man spat out again at the same time the cashier sighed and told her, "I suppose."

"It's against the rules." He wrenched his arm free of the security guard and pointed a finger at Emily. "Just because I'm temporarily skint doesn't mean you won the goods."

"It does if I say it does." The cashier offered Emily an enormous smile, her eyes dancing with mischief. "Unless you'd like us to register the debt and ban you from ever attending again?"

The young man folded his arms, lower lip sticking out like it was swollen. "No, I don't want that."

Emily pulled the cash out of her pocket, folded with the notes all facing the same way. She handed it across, holding her breath while the cashier counted it, only letting it go in a long exhalation when the woman nodded and wrote out a receipt.

"This isn't fair."

"Steady on, mate." The security guard's voice was a high falsetto and Emily had to fight the urge to look twice.

The young man didn't show the same restraint. "Missus take your pair, did she?" He mimed a pair of scissors snipping at crotch level and the cashier turned away in disgust.

"Show him out, Bevan," she said, her lip curling. "Before I feel obliged to take away the rest of his haul."

Emily shuffled toward the door, cradling the puzzle box against her stomach and fighting a triumphant smile. Just to feel the edges against her palm gave her a warm glow.

Capitalism at its worst. Why do you even want such a silly thing?

But she didn't care enough to dwell on the question. Emily even left the wooden toy in her lap as she pulled the seatbelt across her chest. A tap on the window made her jump, and the tattooed arm attached lessened her confidence.

She gave serious thought to just planting her foot and driving away, leaving the man behind her. Then his face lowered, so he grinned at her through the window. He made a winding gesture with his hand as though the push button hadn't taken precedence thirty years ago.

Emily dropped the window a few centimetres. Enough to hear and be heard, not enough to be grabbed. "Can I help you?"

"I need that box," the man said, pointing into Emily's lap. "No joke. How much for it?"

"I'm not selling." Emily pumped her finger onto the button and the window slid back up again.

The man slapped the palm of his hand on the glass. "I'm serious," he shouted, spittle hitting against the window in a spray. "Name your price. I'll sort it out with the bank."

She put the car into gear and revved the engine. With one last, disgusted bang on the bonnet, the man stepped back, scowling as Emily drove past him.

"As if I'd let you go to someone that horrid," she whispered to the puzzle still laying in her lap. If she wasn't still so vigilant about driving, certain at any moment she might have another accident, Emily would have given it a sly pat.

At home, Emily placed the puzzle box on her bedside table. She couldn't resist stroking the wood a few times before leaving it. When she came through into the kitchen, she was astonished to find ten minutes had passed.

"I don't even know why I like it so much," she told Peanut, giving him a pat and listening to his chest roar in response. "But I do."

"What's that?" Cynthia asked as she walked straight through the wall, giving Emily a nasty start. "Have you stashing away goodies from the auction instead of selling them."

"I bought and paid for it, thank you very much."

"Do you have anything exciting planned for the weekend?" Cynthia picked up the ghost cat and gave him a squeeze. "I can't tell you how bored I am."

"The garden's in quite a state." Emily shot it a worried glance, then directed the same expression at her knees. Even with the kneeling pad, it got harder each time to get back up after weeding.

"I think you've misinterpreted my use of the word exciting, Scarface. Isn't it your birthday soon? We could throw a party."

"It's tomorrow and I'm too old to throw anything." Emily opened the fridge, then stared blankly inside the door—forgetting what she'd wanted.

"At least get a nice cake and invite your two friends around to celebrate." Cynthia put her head to one side, scrunching up her nose. "Or is that tally up to three, now?"

"I've got more friends than you, even if you include me in that total."

"Whatever. Women always hated me because I was beautiful."

Emily rolled her eyes. A completely different reason had sprung to her mind.

"Crystal should have something to help you celebrate properly," the ghost continued, unconcerned at the lack of interest. Peanut struggled out of his dead mistress's grip and ran to the pantry, attempting to jump on a tiny potato beetle crawling across the floor.

"You mean music?" Emily leaned against the bench, letting the edge of the formica dig into her lower back. "I used to love a bit of dancing."

"Were you any good at it?"

"It was all slow waving arms and legs when I was growing up. Everyone used dance as a means of self-expression, so notions of being good or bad didn't mean the same thing."

"I'll take it you're bad, then. Anyway, that wasn't the type of aid to celebration I was talking about." She mimed toking on a joint, her eyes half-closed against the imaginary smoke.

"Don't be silly. I'm too old to take up that sort of nonsense. Besides, when my head gets rattled it's capable of giving me a trip all by itself."

Although she'd felt dizzy during the day, Emily had experienced something closer to hallucinations a few weeks ago. The bone fragments in her brain weren't lodged so much as they were free-wheeling.

Emily tried to be sanguine about the situation—there was nothing anybody could do, after all—but it still freaked her out when a dream played out before her eyes while she was still wide awake.

"Cake doesn't sound too bad," she said, laughing as Peanut scampered back to rub against her ankles. "I'm afraid you're in the wrong state to eat it," she told the ghost cat. "But if you want to watch while I scoff the entire thing, you're welcome."

"I need to find a new host," Cynthia grumbled. "Or liven things up by getting my poltergeist on."

"Just stay away from my crockery and glasses if you're going down that route." Emily waggled her finger in the ghost's face. "I can't afford to replace anything at the moment. Not after buying my new treasure."

She'd picked the word up from a friend, Agnes Myrtle, who used it to refer to the objects with sentimental value she'd acquired throughout the years. Even though Emily had let go of her previous collection of object d'art when she first moved from Christchurch to Pinetar, the wooden puzzle reignited the old possessive joy.

Cynthia moved off to examine the new find and Emily tensed until the ghost floated back into the kitchen. "I don't see what's so special about it. Gregory had a bunch of wooden toys when he was younger, and he'd ditch them all if someone brought out the PlayStation."

"You don't need to see what's special. I do and that's why I bought it."

"Okay." Cynthia raised her eyebrows and Emily realised she'd raised her voice.

"Sorry. Things got a bit weird at the auction house."

"Oh?"

"A man won it then couldn't pay for it." Emily shrugged. It didn't sound like a big deal, but her stomach fluttered at the memory of him banging on her window. "He followed me outside after I paid for it, instead."

"He attacked you?"

Emily shook her head. "No. He just offered to buy it from me at any price, then thumped on my car a bit when I didn't agree."

"Living it up, aren't you? If someone acted like that when I was alive, I'd have reported them straight to the police."

"Oh, it wasn't that bad. We just both wanted the same thing and only one of us could have it."

Cynthia furrowed her brow. "And you're talking about the wooden box in your room?"

Her voice was stuffed full of so much confusion that Emily laughed. "Yes."

She fixed herself dinner and sat down in time to watch the news. Cynthia sat beside her, petting Peanut while Emily ate.

"You should at least spring for Netflix," she grumbled as the bulletins gave way to a reality show about doing up houses. "Free-to-air TV is rubbish."

"My wifi bill is high enough without adding shows onto it."

"Go unlimited."

"Go somewhere else and watch telly. Surely, that's the advantage of being a ghost. No one's going to stop you sitting behind them as they binge on Game of Thrones."

"I like it—"

Cynthia closed her mouth with a snap and Emily burst out laughing. If she'd been able to touch the ghost woman, she'd have tickled her silly.

"You like it here. You like me! Go on, admit it."

"You're better than some other places, that's all. I got used to it here." Cynthia stuck out her bottom lip. "Besides, you're holding my cat hostage."

"Hardly. You came back to give him to me, remember?"

As she settled into her bed for the night, Emily picked up the puzzle and worked at it for a few minutes. The rhythm of pushing the innies and the outies until the shape changed was soothing. Emily's eyes glazed over as she concentrated on the feel of the puzzle in her hands.

"For goodness' sake. Leave the thing alone and go to bed. I want to sit outside and watch the stars and I can hardly do that with your light beaming out on me."

Emily shook her head, freeing her mind from the reverie. An hour had disappeared somewhere along the line.

"Whatever," she snapped, offsetting her confusion with a

quick rush of anger. “Why don’t you head on over the rainbow bridge for the night and leave me alone?”

Cynthia ignored her—the benefit of having such a rude and crotchety ghost for a friend was that everything ran off her back.

She sat bolt upright a second later as the puzzle was knocked to the floor. When Emily flicked the light on, Peanut sat on the side table, licking his paws and feigning innocence. The wooden box lay on the floor.

“You’ve got more substance than I give you credit for,” Emily said as she leaned over the side of the bed to pick up the old toy.

The face that stared back from under it came as no real surprise though her heart jumped into Emily’s throat.

“Hello, my new ghost friend,” she said when the hammering settled down to its normal rhythm. “Why don’t you come out from under there and tell me what you need?”

CHAPTER THREE

"One day," Emily said with a yawn wide enough to show off her molars. "A ghost will turn up during the daytime, and I can stop losing sleep."

"I didn't mean... The thing is..."

The female ghost stopped in confusion, her shoulders hunched defensively.

"Don't worry. Just an observation. You don't need to pay me any mind."

"It's better if you don't," Cynthia drawled from the opposite seat.

The new ghost stared at her in wonder, then patted her own tangled locks of hair. "I don't seem to be dressed for the occasion."

"What's that stain all down the front of your dress?" Cynthia leaned forward, squinting. "Or is that some designer's idea of art?"

The ghost plucked the insubstantial material away from her ethereal body. "If I could wash it, believe me, I would." Her voice dropped to a whisper. "It's my blood."

"Ugh." Cynthia jerked back and pulled a face, then held

her hands up as the new arrival launched into an effusive apology. "No, don't worry. It's my fault for asking."

"What's your name?" Emily said, rubbing a hand over her face as she tried to get the conversation back on track.

"Miss Hawthorne," the ghost said, then hunched even further into herself. "I mean, Wanda."

Cynthia snorted in delight. "If that was my first name, I'd go by Miss, too."

"Really?" Emily raised her right eyebrow and stared at her friend. "You're going there? You do remember I saw your *real* name on your coroner's report, though I've been too polite to mention it aloud."

The ghost scowled, crossed her arms, and sat back in the chair. "It's no skin off my nose." Despite her statement, she turned to Wanda. "It was just a casual observation, dear. There's no need to take it to heart."

"Oh, of course," the woman said, nodding her head vigorously. Then a frown mounted her forehead. "Or of course, not. Whichever."

"Do you know why you're still around here?" Emily asked, tapping the table to gain Wanda's attention. Her gaze had been transfixed on Cynthia, similar to how a mouse might stare in awe at a cat.

"I can leave." Wanda jumped to her feet and turned in a circle, searching for the door. "It's no bother. I can come back in the morning, or not. If you don't want to see me again that's fine. I quite understand."

Cynthia's shoulders shook with mirth, but she was considerate enough to clap a hand over her mouth.

"Sit down, Wanda," Emily said in as coaxing a voice as she could manage after eleven o'clock at night. "I meant what you're doing in this world, not in the house. You're welcome here for as long as it takes to get you sorted."

"And since you can speak, you're a vast improvement on the last guest." Cynthia nodded in approval.

Wanda's face remained creased with anxiety, but she sat back down, her back rigid and her butt floating a good inch above the chair. "Only if you're sure."

"I'm sure. Do you remember what happened to you when you died?"

The ghost rubbed at her chest, grimacing as she looked at the large stain. "A car ran me off the road and I wound up hitting the only above-ground electricity pole on the highway running out of town. Bad luck, I suppose."

"It ran you off the road?" Emily cupped the base of her throat and closed her eyes hard to rid them of the sudden image of her own accident. "You mean, deliberately?"

"Oh, no. It was raining," Wanda said, as though that explained everything.

"Most people survive driving in the rain," Cynthia said after leaving a long enough gap with no forthcoming information. "How did a car manage to run you into a pole?"

"They skidded." Wanda shook her head, her lower lip trembling. "It broadsided the rear of my car. There's no way that could've been deliberate."

"Are you sure?" As soon as the words were out of Emily's mouth, she wanted to take them back. The startled look of confusion on her guest's face clearly showed she now doubted herself. "It's just, most of the time when ghosts turn up here, it's because someone killed them."

"I'm not important enough for anyone to want to kill me." Wanda laughed but her eyes were large and sad. "And the other driver got pretty banged up. The collision burst the tank and petrol sprayed everywhere. If it hadn't been for the drizzle, the fire would've killed him as dead as me."

"Your car caught fire?" Emily winced and pulled back

against her chair. She thought that sort of event only happened in Hollywood blockbusters. "How awful."

"It would've been, but I was dead by then." Wanda rubbed at the same position on her chest again, in the middle of her tiny bosom. "The council had a fire danger warning billboard on a pole. My car caught it when I span off the road and lifted the base of it until it caught on the electricity pole."

Suddenly, the large stain spilling down the front of Wanda's dress made perfect sense to Emily. She swallowed a rush of spit, unable to pull her eyes away.

"The warning sign must've been in the red zone, for sure," Cynthia said, the light tone unable to disguise the tremor in her voice. "For everything to catch fire even in the rain."

"I was done like a kebab by the time the emergency department cut me free," Wanda said with a hint of a smile. "Teach me right for wearing my seat belt. My passenger went..." She mimed someone flying through the air.

Emily grabbed a glass of water, unable to sit still with that particular vision knocking around inside her head. "I wonder what it is that brought you to me, then." She touched her fingers to the scar running down the side of her face. "Whatever it is, I hope it's not a guessing game like last time."

"On the other hand," Cynthia said, "with Mr Wilmott you got four deaths sorted for the price of one."

"Go me."

"Am I meant to know what I'm doing here?" Wanda asked, her face pulling into a frown. "Only, I can remember the accident plain as day, but not a lot else."

"Don't worry. It's not as though the afterlife hands you a card with detailed instructions." Cynthia cooed at Peanut who appeared unimpressed. "We're all just playing a guessing game."

"It could be my sister, maybe?"

Emily drank the last of her water and returned to her seat at the table. "What's happened to her?"

"I stored her away for safekeeping," Wanda said, clasping her hands together. "In a little wooden toy. She'll need rescuing from that. Otherwise, her life will be seriously dull."

A minute later, Emily held the puzzle out, retrieved from her bedside cabinet. "Here you go, but I don't know what you mean."

"Oh, it's a witch thing." Wanda waved her hand as though the entire line of questioning was irrelevant. "When I saw the car heading for the pole, I thought I'd better get her out of there. No use both of us getting hurt."

She tried to pick up the puzzle and, when she failed, pulled her mouth down at the corners. "Of course, I didn't know I was going to be staked at the time or I might have cast the incantation for myself."

Cynthia's face sported a snide smile. "You're not one of those, are you?"

"One of whom?"

"The women who hide out in Pinetar forest, pretending that chanting to mushrooms makes them other-worldly."

Wanda chewed on her bottom lip. "I've never chanted anything to fungus in my life."

"But you think you're a witch." Cynthia snorted and shook her head. "I'd rather have the mute Alzheimer's patient back, thanks. At least there was a physical reason for him to be demented."

"I'm not mental," Wanda snapped, with the quick response of someone who'd been accused many times before. "There are more powerful things in this world than most people can see, that's all."

"Sure." Cynthia held up her hand. "Please don't curse me. I'll be shaking in my boots."

"You are sitting at a table close on six months after you

were murdered," Emily said, wrinkling her nose. "And I'm talking to you, so maybe Wanda has a point."

"Oh, please. All this nonsense about witchcraft is just a ruse to sell dried weeds to visiting tourists." Cynthia folded her arms. "One of your lot tried to sell me a love potion when I was first married. Guess how much it was?"

"True witches don't sell love potions, that's against coven law."

"But sticking your sister into a tiny piece of wood, isn't?"

"It was an emergency."

Cynthia reached over, picked up the puzzle, and knocked it against the edge of the table. "Hello? Are you in there?"

Emily snatched it out of her hands while Wanda looked on, open-mouthed.

"How can you do that? When I tried to touch it, my hands went straight through it."

"Cynthia's a poltergeist," Emily explained. "Our best guess is she's able to harness those powers through the magic of being continually bad-tempered."

The ghost in question sniffed. "It's by using my energy properly. I'd show you how, but since you can just use witchcraft, there wouldn't be any point."

"That's not how—"

Emily held up a hand. "Cynthia, stop sniping at her for a minute." She turned to Wanda. "I want to understand."

"I cast a spell and put my sister in the puzzle for safekeeping. You'll need to release her spirit back to the world in order to free her." Wanda reached for the toy again and hissed when her hand passed straight through it. "I can't do it like this."

"Can you tell us what to do?"

"You'll need a book of spells. It'll probably be back at my flat. You just read out the incantation and the power residing within the book will work its magic and release her. As long as it's performed within a calendar year of the entrapment, she'll be perfectly fine."

"That should give us plenty of time." Emily's eyes blinked, not wanting to reopen. "Will you be okay here, while I head on back to bed? It's Saturday tomorrow, so we can get started nice and early."

"Sure. Whenever you feel up to it." Wanda bit on the side of her thumbnail, frowning at the table.

"Yes, you get your rest," Cynthia said with a slight edge to her smile. "I've loads more questions to ask our new ghost pal, here."

IT WAS nice to wake up, knowing there was a new ghost in the house, but without its face hanging a centimetre away when Emily opened her eyes. She took a leisurely time getting out of bed, lying back against the pillows while her mind figured out a plan for the day.

Barring unforeseen eventualities, she should be home again with the spell book in hand by midmorning at the very latest. She couldn't imagine even the longest ritual would take more than an hour or two to perform. That left her free by midday.

Maybe Cynthia was right, and she should do something for today to treat herself. While they were out and about this morning, she'd pop in to see if Crystal was free. A spot of lunch in the Honeysuckle Café sounded nice.

"Morning all. Did you dig up any new goodies overnight that I should know about?"

Cynthia had a flush to her cheeks that indicated she'd been up to no good, but Wanda was sitting and waiting with equanimity. Whatever trouble Cynthia had tried to stir up mustn't have eventuated as she'd planned.

"Wanda, it's good to see you again. Could you scoot over to the sofa while I have my breakfast? Peanut likes to sit in that chair and stare at my food. He gets lost in happy memories of when he used to eat."

"I saw him trying to play outside with a field mouse the other day." Cynthia stretched her arms up and pointed vaguely at the back yard. "Even without the means to hold it still, he had it pinned with his fiery gaze."

Peanut wandered into the kitchen at the sound of the toaster and looked mildly suspicious when they burst into chuckles. He ignored them—mere humans that they were—and padded the cushion of the chair Wanda had vacated until he had it to his liking.

"I used to have a familiar," Wanda said, her voice catching. "The cutest wee black cat. One Christmas I brought her a plush mouse as a plaything, and it was the best present ever."

"Peanut's far too sophisticated to be content with a cheap toy." Cynthia blew a kiss at her cat across the table.

"So was Dark Spirits. I meant the box the plushy came in. My cat curled up in that thing until the sides gave way from use."

Even at the word box, Peanut's ears perked up, and he turned around to stare at the supposed witch with new interest.

As Emily sat down with her breakfast, a knock sounded on the door.

"I thought all your friends were already here?" Cynthia said with a curious stare.

Emily flapped a hand at her, part of her hoping somebody had sent her a birthday present via courier. If so, that would be a great start to the day.

Instead, she opened the door to find her brother Harvey on the doorstep, with two boxes and a suitcase.

"What?" Emily asked in confusion as he waved goodbye to the taxi reversing along her driveway.

"I've come to stay for a few days," he announced with a cheerful grin, as though this wasn't the last thing in the world she'd expect. "I knew you wouldn't mind."

CHAPTER FOUR

"I could've sworn you mentioned this place had a second bedroom," Harvey said as he finished looking around the house. His insistence on checking out her new 'digs' seemed on the edge of insinuating she'd told him an untruth.

Emily sat at the kitchen table, her mind still struggling to keep up with the new arrival. She couldn't remember telling Harvey anything about her new home. The last she recalled speaking to him was at the hospital, a long way from recovery.

"Never mind," he announced, planting himself on a seat opposite Emily. The chair where Peanut was seated.

Or had been. Emily watched the ghost cat sprint to the pantry to hide behind the wooden shutters.

"I'm happy to use the couch as a bed for a while. My back might grumble for a few days, but it does that often enough as it is."

"What's happening to your place?" Emily placed her palms flat on the table as though she needed to balance. "Don't you have the final exams coming up?"

Harvey had been a lecturer at the university the last time she checked but Emily guessed from the expression of shock on his face that had been a long time ago.

"I've been working at a surveyance firm, you know that." Harvey shrugged. "I decided to take a break from it for a while. Get back to my roots and all that. Every time I look up from my desk, my coworkers are a decade younger." He ran a hand through his grey and thinning hair. "It gets a bit tiring trying to find some common areas of interest."

"How's Marie doing?"

Her brother swivelled on his chair to look out into the back yard. "This is quite a neat little set-up you've got here. Do you own it outright?"

Emily frowned. "It's paid for. It's quite a downsize from my last house so I was able to get rid of the mortgage. Plus, housing is cheaper here."

"Not a bad idea. I've been thinking of doing something similar."

"If you've given up your job, you'll have to."

Harvey waved a hand at her. "That's just a sabbatical. I wanted a bit of space to sort myself out. Midlife crisis and all that."

Cynthia laughed from the lounge. "How long does your brother expect to live? Until he's a hundred and fifty?"

Emily did a quick calculation in her head. She turned fifty-three today, which put Harvey at sixty. "Isn't it a bit late for all that?"

"Never too late." Harvey winked at her and Emily pulled a face.

"It is if you've got retirement just around the corner. Unless you're all set?" She raised her eyebrows.

But Harvey just flapped his hand at her again. "I'm taking a few months off, not the rest of my life. Work'll still be there when I sort myself out."

"How long have you been at the surveyor's?" Emily stared hard at the table as she tried to remember any conversation about him changing work. The problem was, they spoke so seldom, all their chats were hazy.

"Coming up on five years but I don't want to talk about work."

Harvey reached across the table and took Emily's hands in his own. They were rough—more fitting to a manual labourer than a man who'd spent most of his life in various office chairs.

"Tell me what you've been up to. I haven't seen you since you were in the hospital."

Emily withdrew from his grasp and stood up, putting the kettle on to boil. "Oh, you know. I've just been getting used to Pinetar again and settling into work at the shop."

"An op-shop, I think you said."

"Yeah, it's a charity shop for the local battered woman's shelter." She shrugged. "It keeps me occupied."

As she walked to the table, Emily's numb foot twisted, and she stumbled. Harvey frowned. "I thought you were all better when the hospital let you go."

Despite her embarrassment, she burst into laughter. The roving bone fragments, illiteracy, and growing neuropathy were so far from 'all better' it was hard to fathom.

"I'm alive, there's that," she said. "But I have trouble with a lot of things still."

"But your head's all sorted, right?"

Emily frowned down at her shaking fingers. In the corner of her eye, she watched Wanda watching her. "Not really. I still can't read or write."

Harvey sat back, clapping his hands together. "Sounds like me staying here will sort both of us, then. If you need me to read something or write an email, you let me know."

"What about Marie?"

Emily glanced up in time to see a look of sorrow pass in and out of her elder brother's eyes.

"She won't be joining me." Harvey cleared his throat and stared out the window. "In fact, we called it quits a few years ago. I didn't like to say with your—" He waved his hand at Emily, presumably referencing her car accident.

"I'm so sorry." She fumbled for the right words to say, feeling aghast. "I had no idea."

"It's fine. What's done is done, hey? No use dwelling in the past or thinking about what might have been."

Harvey leapt to his feet and moved to the bench as the kettle whistled it was done. He opened cupboards and pulled out drawers, making both him and Emily a cup of coffee.

"I'm sorry to turn up here, unannounced," he said, coming back to the table with the full mugs. "Only, it just occurred to me on the spur of the moment, then I didn't want to ring in case you told me to stay away." He took a sip and grimaced, then took another. "I miss my little sister."

Emily flushed, knowing what he said was right. She warmed her hands on the mug, staring at the swirl of bubbles from where he'd stirred in two sugars. "Did you want to do anything while you were here? It must be an age since you visited Pinetar."

He nodded in agreement. "I haven't been back since I left the first time. Thought I might just wander about this afternoon and reacclimate myself, maybe catch up with a few old friends. Is the old tavern still going?"

"It'd survive the apocalypse. I'll grab you a set of house keys." She walked past Wanda and ignored Cynthia's cynical smile. Peanut was curled up in a patch of sun on her bed. Her unmade bed.

The spare keys were in the top drawer of an old chest stored inside the wardrobe. As Emily pulled them out, she closed her eyes, listening to the sounds of her brother moving about in the kitchen.

"He can't stay here," Cynthia said, so close to Emily that she made her hairs stand on end. "You won't be able to last more than a few days before you talk back to one of us in his presence, then he'll think you're mad and lock you up."

With her ear attuned to make sure her brother remained in the other room, Emily whispered, "Your family believes me, along with Crystal and Sergeant Winchester. None of them locked me up."

"Mainly due to *my* performance. If it'd just been you, spouting nonsense about ghosts, it wouldn't have been that easy."

Emily coloured as she remembered her first trip into the police station. Despite a new level of respect being afforded by the officers there, the memory of their original scornful laughter hadn't lost its potency. "I'm sure he won't stay too long."

"Will you still be able to release my sister?"

With a sigh, Emily turned to face Wanda. Again, she listened to ensure her brother was a safe distance away before answering, "Yes. I'll just get Harvey settled and then we'll go." She pointed a finger at Cynthia. "And I'd appreciate if you could all keep your mouths buttoned until then."

Without awaiting a response, she jingled the spare set of keys in her hand and walked back to the kitchen. "Here you go. I've got a few errands to run this morning, so I'll leave you alone for a few hours."

Harvey was standing at the sink, so Emily couldn't read his expression, but she could see the slump in his shoulders.

"It's my birthday, today, so I'll pick up a nice cake while I'm in town and we can celebrate together tonight unless you have other plans."

"I'm a dolt." Harvey turned and gave her a bearhug that

went on far too long in Emily's estimation. "I completely forgot today was the day. Fifty-four, isn't it? I'll shout you somewhere to celebrate."

"Fifty-three and I'm good just spending it at home for exactly that reason. Don't let the c—" Emily broke off and blushed, aware she'd been about to warn him not to let the cat he couldn't see out of the house. As though doors would stop Peanut, anyway.

Harvey raised an eyebrow, but Emily hurried along the hall and out the front door before he could ask.

"Thank goodness, that's done," Cynthia said. "Watching you and your brother interact is painful, to say the least."

"I'm sorry if I'm a nuisance." Wanda wrung her hands together as she hovered by the car.

"You're fine," Emily reassured her. "Now, let's go and fetch this spell book and get your sister sorted out."

"I DON'T KNOW anyone of that name," the woman who answered the door said, shaking her head to remove any doubt. She cast an anxious glance at Emily, then shuffled back half a step.

"Lionel?" The shout could have penetrated through steel. "You know anyone of the name Hawthorne?"

A muffled response came back, so low Emily couldn't catch the words and Wanda appeared nonplussed.

"When was that?" the woman asked, then disappeared into the house. A few seconds later, she returned, dragging a man by the sleeve of his cardigan. "He'll tell you, love. I'm getting back to my breakfast. My eggs'll be stone cold."

Emily tried to apologise, but the woman had gone. The man—presumably the husband—squinted through thick lenses. The prescription was so extreme his eyes overflowed the frames, close to cartoonish. With a diamond-check fair isle vest topped with the thick texture of a cable knit orange cardigan, he looked like a throwback to the seventies. The leather elbow patches made Emily smile.

"They lived here before us, but I never met either of them," he said, pushing his glasses up by the nosepiece. He squinted harder, and the frames slid down before catching in the wrinkles on his nose. "Both young girls, in their twenties, I think. We got loads of mail through before I managed to convince the post office we weren't them."

"Do you know what happened to them?" Emily shifted her weight from foot to foot, a slow dance to keep the feeling in her toes alive. "What made them move away from here?"

"Oh, it was terrible." The man risked a quick glance over his shoulder, then pulled the door closed, with him standing on the outside. "A car accident out on the main highway. One of them drove into a pole or something and was killed outright. The other girl, she's still in the hospital."

"In hospital?"

Emily's voice contained more surprise than it should, and the man jerked backwards as though she'd accused him of something. "Yes, that's right. Ask at the main desk of the place if you don't believe me."

"Sorry, I just wasn't..." Emily trailed off and shook her head, frowning down at her feet.

"Okay, I get a bit sensitive about the subject. It's an awful business but there's nothing worrying will do to restore her to health. As far as I've heard, she's on life support but there's nothing going on." The man leaned further out, the scent of bacon wafting on the gentle wave of his exhalations. "Up here, like." He tapped the side of his head.

"Oh, no. That's truly sad, especially at her age."

"Car accidents are nasty, that's for sure." He drew back a

step, his hand fumbling for the door. "If you don't need anything else…?"

"Thanks for your time." Emily nodded and turned her back, avoiding Wanda's distraught gaze. She kept her eyes fixed on the cracked concrete of the driveway all the way back to the car and concentrated more attention than was needed on fastening her seatbelt.

"It's not what you think. My sister is still in the box, it's just her body needs to be somewhere while her mind is gone. Even the Supreme can't turn something into nothing just because it's inconvenient."

Emily shrugged. "I wasn't doubting you, but we might as well pay a visit to the hospital before we go any further."

Wanda nodded, twiddling her thumbs together in her lap. "Do you think those people put my stuff into storage? If I can't locate that book, then it won't matter what's happening to my sister's body."

Before her common sense kicked in, Emily reached out to give Wanda a reassuring pat. When her hand sank into the ghost's insubstantial form instead, she cast a pleading glance at Cynthia.

"There, there," Mrs Pettigrew said, leaning forward to stroke the ghost's shoulder. "The man camped out in your old house is right. There's no use worrying about the things you can't change. If we can find out where your stuff is now, we will."

It didn't sound very reassuring to Emily, but Wanda grabbed onto the words like a lifeline. "You're right. Of course, you're right. Let's get to the hospital and then work on a plant to get my sister restored and out of there."

CHAPTER FIVE

Emily suppressed a shiver as the lift rose, the steel ropes groaning. Cynthia had pointed to the button to press, though with only three floors she could have hazarded a guess. Her recuperation in hospital was now eight months behind her, but the three-month-long stay had left an impression in her mind, drafted with indelible ink.

The smells brought back the hardest memories. The squeak of rubber-soled shoes on linoleum floated others to the surface. As her chest tightened and breathing became a luxury, it took all Emily's resolve to stay in place.

If Wanda and Cynthia hadn't been there with her, she would have wrenched the elevator doors open, and fled.

"It'd be quicker to walk the stairs," Mrs Pettigrew muttered as the bell dinged for their floor.

Emily lifted her eyebrows but didn't comment. If they'd taken the manual option, she'd still be struggling up the first flight. Being able to float around wherever she pleased had cut down on Cynthia's capacity to judge other's limitations.

As the doors opened, a figure pushed inside, and Emily gave a cry of surprise. Common courtesy dictated the person waiting should step back to let her out, but she recovered and shook her head in recrimination as she walked into the corridor.

It was only as the lift doors closed that she recognised the young man, adorned with tattoos, who'd she'd encountered at the auction house a day ago. He was staring at the floor, grimacing, and Emily turned away before he could look up and recognise her.

"Rude," Cynthia said, giving a snort. "I thought Gregory could be bad but compared to the rest of his generation, I raised a proper gentleman."

"You did," Emily agreed. With every conversation she shared with Gregory at work, she liked the young man a little more.

"This is the one." Wanda stopped by a door and stuck her head inside the room. "It has a sign out saying not to enter until you check with the desk staff.

Emily nodded her understanding, not wanting to risk her voice. She clutched her elbows in each hand while trotting along the corridor. Speed made her hip ache, but the physical pain was easier than the damage caused by multiple withdrawals from her memory bank.

"Miss Hawthorne is going through her morning routine at the moment," the desk nurse said with a smile. "She'll be finished up in ten minutes or so. There's a room down the end of the corridor if you'd like to wait."

Emily traced the path with her eyes but stayed standing by the desk. "There was a young man just here, covered with tattoos and with some burn scars on one arm. Could you tell me who he was visiting?"

The nurse's expression didn't change as she stared back, not speaking for a full minute. "Why don't you ask him yourself, if you're acquainted?"

"Oh, hm. I was just wondering. I don't know him that

well."

"So, you wouldn't like me to give him a call when you leave and tell him everything you got up to here?"

Point taken. The shame of asking something she shouldn't compounded her nervousness. After a swallow that took all her concentration, Emily mouthed her thanks and followed the directions to the waiting room at the end of the hall.

"What on earth does a morning routine entail?" Cynthia asked, hands on her hips. She stared at the coffee machine with a petulant frown.

"I really don't want to know," Emily said, her vocal cords as stiff as concrete.

One glance at the window told her not to bother seeking a view. They were on the third floor, and the cleaners obviously didn't get around this side of the complex much. Dust from the everlasting Christchurch rebuild caked the glass, turning it opaque.

A trail of liquid gleamed on the floor, but Emily turned her face away from that, too, not wanting to inspect it enough to determine its origin. The sharp tang of antiseptic warred with a floral air freshener plugged into a nearby socket.

"I might go and check on her, first." Wanda retreated a few steps towards the doorway. "See that they're taking care of her."

Emily opened her mouth to warn her not to—nothing good would come of sneaking in before they should—then she closed it again with a snap as a fellow visitor came into the room. She nodded at the new arrival instead and pulled at her lips with her right hand, a game to stop her accidentally talking to her invisible companions.

"She's asking for trouble," Cynthia commented with a raised eyebrow.

Why don't you go and stop her, then?

Emily settled for a shake of her head, clamping her lips even tighter together.

"You here for family?" the stranger asked, a forced smile testing the muscles of her jaw.

"A friend." Emily returned her gaze to the window, not wanting to engage in conversation. Even when she heard the woman sniffing, she didn't turn around to look.

I'd rather be anywhere but here.

And why should she be? Emily jerked as the thought hit and clutched her handbag tighter. This was her birthday and so far, it had brought nothing but trouble and upset. She should leave, go get that cake and spend the afternoon at the beach, or the roller derby if her co-worker Pete was competing today.

"Sheryl's ready for you, now," a nurse said from the doorway. Emily waited for the other woman to respond, then realised the words were directed at her.

See? You haven't even bothered to find out the name of Wanda's sister. This is a foolish idea.

Of course, it was foolish. Emily struggled to her feet and followed the nurse out of the room. It was just as foolish to believe she could see ghosts or sort out their troubles so they could move onto the next realm.

"Do you think they deliberately choose this shade of pastel green to encourage patients out of here?" Cynthia asked with a delicate curl of her upper lip.

A pity that sometimes they came back from that realm and took up residence in her house.

"She can hear you," the nurse said as they reached Sheryl Hawthorne's room. Wanda hovered inside, near the window. "Don't worry about sounding silly if you talk aloud. It'll be a comfort to the patient and none of the nurses are listening." She gave a laugh that boomed out from her abdomen. "We've got far too much work to eavesdrop on chats with our long-term residents."

"Hello, Sheryl," Emily said dutifully, sitting beside the bed and taking the young woman's hand in hers. The skin had a dull shine and felt smooth to the touch. As she stared at the limp fingers, fearful memories prodded at her battered brain, trying to escape.

"I don't know what this visit is meant to tell you." Cynthia leaned over the patient, staring with intensity at the woman's closed eyes. "Boo!"

No response. Even the heart-rate monitor just continued its steady beeping.

"It'd be nice if you could behave yourself while you're in here," Emily told the ghost, keeping her eyes fixed on the comatose woman in case the nurse came sneaking back. "Would you like to tell your sister anything, Wanda?"

"It's no use talking to that thing." Wanda had stayed in position, a metre and a half back from the bed. "It's not my sister. I told you her essence is stuck in the puzzle box." She waved a hand over the still body. "This is just an empty container."

The description was so apt, Emily felt sorrow wash over her. Like a tin that all the humanity had been tipped out of, its purpose finished as soon as the contents spilled.

"I thought I was saving her," Wanda said, her face flushed with sadness. "But I can't get her out and all our stuff's missing…" She gulped as the full import of the situation hit her.

"We'll find your spell book," Emily said in as comforting a tone as she could manage. If the outer hallways had creeped her out with their memories, the sterility of the room was pushing her close to madness.

"Hocus Pocus." Cynthia sniffed and prodded Sheryl's lifeless body. "If her head's been banged up in a car accident, no ritual's going to bring her back."

Emily's fingers crept up to trace the scar on her cheek, a shudder worming the length of her spine. She pulled the puzzle box out of her handbag and set it on the bedside table, one finger resting lightly on the top. "We'll try, whether you're going to help or not."

The heart-rate monitor caught a faster rhythm. As Emily stared at the flashing numbers on the screen, she could see them changing shape, even if she couldn't interpret the meaning.

"Move it closer," Cynthia demanded.

For a second, Emily couldn't work out what she meant, then followed the ghost's nod to the puzzle box. With a frown, she placed it on the pillow instead, still keeping her forefinger touched to the varnished surface.

The devices leapt again, the audible trace sounding a second before the screen started to flash a faster beat.

"Whatever else is going on, your sister really responds to that toy," Cynthia said with a sniff, tilting her head in the slightest concession that Wanda might be telling the truth.

"I wonder how it's connected?" Emily placed the puzzle right above Sheryl's heart, nestling it down into the stiff hospital covers. "Perhaps we can get whatever's trapped here back into her—"

The machines sounded a shrill warning. Confused, Emily pulled back, dropping the wooden toy into her bag and holding her hands up to either side as a nurse rushed into the room.

"Cardiac arrest," the nurse said, staring at the array of flashing lights on the different sections of the machine.

"Are you going to call the crash cart?" Emily said when the nurse made no further movements, and the woman shook her head.

"This patient's DNR. If you want to say goodbye, now would be the time to do it."

"DNR?" Wanda asked, her voice tight with panic.

"Do not resuscitate," Cynthia explained with a shrug. "I guess your sister's a goner. Unless you've got a magic spell up your sleeve."

CHAPTER SIX

"No," Wanda shouted. "You have to do something." She stepped forward, her hands plunging through her sister's chest as she tried to pump Sheryl's failing heart back to life.

The panic was contagious. Emily's own heart skipped a beat, then thumped like a fist pounding inside her chest as it caught up again. "Help her," she said to the nurse, her voice rising in tone and volume. "You can't just stand there and let her die."

But the nurse shook her head, standing firm. "We can't," she said in a voice so calm it edged into serenity. "The patient's family made it quite clear there were to be no rescue attempts."

"What family?" Wanda shouted. She walked up to the nurse, yelling the question into her face. "I'm her only family and I say to revive her, right now."

The monitor gave another faint beep as Sheryl's pulse caught, then faltered again.

"Save her. I'm ordering you right now as next of kin. If you let her die, I'll have the police charge you with murder!"

As if she caught an echo of the distressed ghost's words, the nurse took a step back, sweeping a hand over her face. "She isn't feeling any pain. It's time to let her go."

With Wanda yelling in one ear and even Cynthia appearing disturbed, Emily leapt onto the bed. She'd been the office Health and Safety officer at her accounting firm for ten years running. Though her first aid certificate might have lapsed a year ago, she still remembered what to do.

The nurse was shouting now, but over the cacophony of noise that Wanda and Cynthia produce, Emily couldn't understand her. She felt along Sheryl's sternum and counted four finger widths up from the base. With her hands clasped together, she leaned her whole weight onto the supine woman's chest.

Her mind couldn't remember the song they'd been taught to sing to keep the right rhythm, so Emily just went as fast as she could. The nurse gripped her shoulder, but she threw her weight back to get rid of the grip and continued.

The tube inserted in Sheryl's mouth meant Emily didn't need to worry about pausing to give breaths. As her arms shook from the strain of pumping, she concentrated solely on the movement, hoping the faint crackle reverberating from the patient wasn't a breaking rib.

"I'm calling the police. This is straight assault," the nurse cried, loud enough to be heard over Wanda's screams of encouragement. "Stop it right now!"

"If you touch me," Emily struggle to say between pants, "it's also an assault."

The nurse retreated. Emily could sense her standing behind her, but at least she didn't grab for her again. The rhythm of her compressions continued, sweat forming from the continuing exertion, her breath hot in her lungs.

A beep came from the monitor again, then a frantic series of them, chasing each other in a pattern far too quick to be healthy. Emily gasped, a sob caught in the back of her throat as she continued to pump her arms, nearing exhaustion.

How long had it been? One minute? Ten? She was so dreadfully weak these days, Emily couldn't be sure. Her mind was swamped with the command to keep going, to save the woman's life.

A spurt of electricity zapped past her face. Behind her, a woman screamed.

Emily turned, flicking her sweat sodden curls out of her eyes to see. Wanda held an arm out, stiff as a board, pointing her forefinger straight at the machines hooked to her sister.

With an instinct for survival, Emily launched herself off Sheryl, getting caught in the covers as she fell to the side of the bed. An arch of electricity crackled through the air, filling it with the strange scent of ozone.

Sheryl's body jumped. The nurse had backed so far across the room she was almost out the door. She screamed again.

Footsteps pounded along the hallway as Emily untangled herself from the bedding. She stood just in time for another nurse to burst into the room.

"She's a witch," the first nurse shrieked, pointing a shaking finger at Emily.

Cynthia leaned over Sheryl's body, dragged with the bedding so it was now at the edge of the bed. "That was actually quite impressive," she said with a nod to Wanda. "Perhaps you are magic, after all."

Emily staggered back a few steps as the room filled with more people, collapsing onto the windowsill as though it were a seat.

"Call the police," the first nurse managed to shout. "And don't let that woman leave here, she's under a citizen's arrest."

Her finger pointed straight at Emily.

SERGEANT WINCHESTER SHOOK his head and sighed. "It's not a joke. What you did is considered battery and is punishable under the law."

Although Emily hadn't been able to stop the nurse calling law enforcement, she had managed to convince her to contact the Pinetar station rather than Christchurch central. If she hadn't, she might have been having a very different experience right now.

"But I revived her!" Emily bit her lip, chewing away the smile that had been sitting there. Although the police had collected her from the hospital and transported her to the station without delay, the entire incident seemed backwards.

"You went against the family's wishes." The sergeant pressed his fingertips up to his temple and winced. "When there's a DNR in place, any attempt to revive the patient is considered an assault against the person."

"Then the entire matter is ridiculous." Emily sat back in her chair, tipping her chin up in defiance. "Besides, I'd like to know what family these wishes belong to. As far as I know, the only family Sheryl Hawthorne possessed was a sister who died in a car accident. Who's been making these orders?"

Sergeant Winchester shrugged. "I don't know. I'm just passing along the information the hospital gave me. Unless you have some evidence to say they're mistaken, then I'd rather concentrate on what to do with you, than who is making the decisions as Miss Hawthorne's medical proxy."

"What you should do is send me home." Emily massaged her right shoulder, which was throbbing. "It feels like I've gone a few rounds in the boxing ring and with someone in a seriously different weight class."

"It's not that easy. We'll have to pass the case along to the prosecution service, but they might want to make a show of you. It's not just Miss Hawthorne who's affected by your actions." He tapped a pen on his blotter and stared hard at Emily. "The patient you assaulted is an organ donor."

Emily's indignation disappeared as though sucked out by a giant vacuum. "I didn't know that."

"What I'd like to understand is how you knew this young woman at all. Why were you at the hospital today? The nursing staff said they'd never seen you there before."

"I was asked to visit her by a friend. They wanted to ensure Sheryl was being treated okay."

"A live friend or a dead one?"

Emily's gaze fell on a rubber plant, perched against the wall. The tips of its leaves were browning. "Does it matter?"

"Probably not." The sergeant leaned back in his chair, swinging it back and forth so his foot bumped up against the inside of his desk well. "The hospital told me there's a little girl waiting on a heart transplant. Without a donor, she mightn't make it through the night."

"Then they're pulling at your heart strings, trying to make their point." Emily folded her arms across her chest. "It's just as likely the little blip in Miss Hawthorne's heart rhythm was caused by the excitement of our visit, and if we'd never gone there at all, everything would've turned out the same."

"*Our* visit, huh?"

A flush spread up Emily's throat. "Just a slip of the tongue. If I wanted to find out who's making medical decisions on Sheryl's behalf, how would I find that out?"

"You wouldn't. It's private."

A beep sounded from Sergeant Winchester's computer and his attention turned to the screen for a minute. "You've got a reprieve," he said, standing. "We've got an urgent call out. Get home and don't leave town and I'll let you know if we're pressing charges."

"Like I have anywhere to go." Emily stood up, disappearing out of the sergeant's line of sight before he changed his mind. As she stood outside, blinking in the sun, she realised her car was still back at the hospital.

She pulled the phone out of her pocket, frowning as the two police cars in the car park took off with a squeal of tyres.

Agnes Myrtle from the Stoneybrook Acres Retirement Village had programmed in a number for the local Uber driver, bypassing the app so she wouldn't have to pay the Uber rates. After arranging for a pickup, Emily sat on the bench outside the station.

"Happy birthday to me," she sang off-tune for the benefit of her ghostly companions. "This is what you get for turning fifty-three."

"Forget your self-pity for a moment," Cynthia said with a flap of her hands. "I want to know how you got lightning to shoot out of your hands." She turned to Wanda, the earlier lip curls and dismissive shakes of her head replaced by an expression of awe. "And if you can teach that trick to me."

"It's not a trick." Wanda stared at her shaking hands, picking at a fingernail. "That's just some elemental magic. You've either got the knack of using it"—she risked a quick glance at Cynthia—"or you don't."

If Wanda thought that would be enough to get Cynthia off her back, she was in for another think. While Emily waited for her car to arrive, more muscles adding their voices to the chorus of pain with every passing second, Mrs Pettigrew cajoled, harangued, and finally threatened Wanda to give up her secrets.

"You can hardly kill her again," Emily whispered as a car pulled up alongside the station. The driver waved while the large cat perching on his shoulder stared. "And it'd be nice if everyone kept quiet on this journey. I'm in enough pain without adding a headache from your yelling to the list."

Her plea went ignored. By the time Frank Libertyman—the driver—had dropped Emily at her car, the two ghosts had declared full-out war. Where Wanda had been painfully shy earlier in the day, the visit to her sister appeared to have replaced her spine with steel.

"Could you two please cool it," Emily pleaded again. "Our focus now should be working out where the spell book might have ended up. I presume it was sold at auction the same as the puzzle box. It'll take a lot to sort through all the potential buyers and I can't concentrate with you squabbling."

"I'm not," Cynthia said, appearing disgusted. "All I want to know is how to do a few spells. It's not like I can get into any trouble with them. Not now I'm dead."

"If you wanted to learn about witchcraft, you should've enquired while you were still alive." Wanda sat back, arms crossed, nose up in the air. "It's not my place to teach you."

"Maybe, if we find the spell book, you can teach yourself."

Emily said the words just to gain a bit of peace, but Cynthia latched onto the idea. "Great. Let's do that, then. Will the auction house be open?"

"Not on Saturday. They open again for auctions on Monday." Emily turned the corner, pulling into her street. The usual relief she felt at coming home after a long day's work was missing and not just because it was only midday.

"Looks like your brother's made himself at home," Cynthia said with a laugh as the driveway came into view. A pile of old boxes not yet unpacked from when Emily moved in six months ago lay on the driveway, right where she wanted to park the car.

"Hasn't he just," Emily muttered under her breath.

CHAPTER SEVEN

Harvey gave Emily a wave as she got out of the car, a wide grin decorating his face. "I hope you don't mind. I got a hankering for some old-fashioned hokey-pokey biscuits but couldn't find any baking stuff in the kitchen."

"And you thought dragging all my possessions onto the driveway would somehow help?" Emily shielded her face from the sun with her hand, squinting at her older brother as though he'd gone mad.

"There weren't any labels. I thought if I stacked them out here, rather than trying to squint at them in the dingy garage, I'd be able to work out what was in what."

Emily shifted her hands to her hips, deciding it was more important to display her frustration than prevent temporary blindness. "I can't read remember? What good do you think labels would do me?"

Harvey turned bright pink and stared at his feet. "Um, yeah. I forgot. How do you know what's in what, then?"

"The pictures." Emily pointed to a small drawing on the side of one box. It had a bookshelf sketched on it. "That's all the books from my old house. I couldn't work out what to keep or throw out, so I just packed them all up. You're welcome to go through them if you want some of Mum and Dad's old favourites."

She moved closer as Harvey wrote something on the top of the box. After tilting one up, she tapped her finger on another drawing. "This is the one with all the kitchen stuff." She shrugged. "I haven't felt much like baking since I moved in."

"What's this drawing meant to be?" Harvey stared at it in confusion.

"It's a set of cutlery," Emily said, glaring at him in a full-on challenge. "Anyone could see that."

He pulled his mouth down at the corner, but she was busy with the next box. Funny how she could open and sort through a dozen or more in a single day at the charity shop, but she hadn't yet got these organised yet.

"This one is gardening equipment." Emily pushed the box back towards the garage. No need to get that out, not with winter about to take a firm grip. "And this one is old ornaments."

"You kept those?" Harvey took a step back, his eyebrows crawling halfway up his forehead in surprise. "I didn't think you celebrated Christmas."

"I don't." Emily sighed. "It seemed wrong to chuck them out when Mum took so much care over the years to keep them in one piece."

Harvey pulled up one flap and dragged out a tangle of tinsel. It looked more like sad, metallic string than the vibrant decoration it had once been. All the feathers of shiny green had dropped off like the pine needles of its living counterpart.

"Yeah, better keep those for the next generation," he scoffed, pushing the box shut again.

"What next generation?" Emily kicked her foot against

the box. "Unless you've got a love child somewhere you neglected to tell me about, I think that ship's well and truly sailed."

"Hey, never say never." Harvey stretched out his back, groaning. "Cary Grant had a child when he was over a hundred, or something like that."

"In his early sixties, I think you'll find." Emily nudged her brother's shoulder. "Given the trouble you had finding a hot wife when you were young, I don't rate your chances nowadays."

A cloud sailed across Harvey's face and was gone. "There's a bit of life left me in me, yet," he said, patting his butt with a satisfied grin.

"How about you put it to good use and move these back inside?"

"Sure thing, boss." Harvey tossed her a salute and began to move everything back where it had been.

With a shake of her head, Emily walked inside and immediately wished the police had locked her up at the station.

A pile of dishes sat by the sink. No, not just beside it, inside it as well. A spill of something that had started off liquid but long since hardened into cement decorated the cabinet door beneath the bench. A snail's trail of the same substance marked a path from the stovetop to the sink.

Just pretend you didn't see it! Go and sit on the sofa as you planned.

"Even Gregory never got our kitchen into a state like this," Cynthia said, following the words with an appreciative whistle.

"That's because you had a housekeeper."

"Ha! A lot of good that did me."

"Holy moly." Wanda moved up to inspect the sink at close quarters then moved away, her lips and nose wrinkling in a moue of distaste.

"Don't worry about the dishes," Harvey announced, sailing in through the front door with an armful of supplies. "I'll clean everything up once I finish baking. It'll be spick and span again by the time the biscuits have cooled."

"I've heard that before," Cynthia said, purring with satisfaction. "You better nip this nonsense in the bud otherwise, he'll just keep making a mess of things. You mark my words."

Emily opened her mouth, unsure if she was about to unleash a tirade or a sentence of acceptance when the phone rang. The actual phone, in the hallway, rather than her smartphone on which any normal person would call her.

"Hello?" she said in a brusque voice, hoping it was a salesperson so she could mash the off button and slam the phone back into its cradle.

"Emily! I'm so glad I caught you. How do you fancy being an audience member tonight?"

She took a few moments to place the familiar voice.

"Pete?"

"Of course, it's Pete. Who else would invite you to the roller derby?"

Emily laughed. "Is that what you're doing?"

"It is." Pete dropped his voice a few notches of volume. "It's Gregory's debut, but it slipped my mind to invite you last week like I said I would."

"Well, if it's Gregory, I have to come, don't I? Whereabouts and what time?"

"Meet us at the charity shop and we'll give you a lift," Pete said, his voice full of relief. "Bring a friend or two along. There's plenty of room."

"In your car, or in the hall?"

"Both. I can take three and Gregnado can fit a few in his dad's car."

"Gregnado, eh?" Emily glanced up to see Harvey staring at her with an amused smile on his face. She turned, blocking him with her shoulder as though the phone cared who saw it. "What's your stage name?"

"For Pete's Sake," her friend answered, then guffawed. "Not the most original."

"What time?" she repeated, dropping her voice lower as her brother continued to stare with interest.

"Four thirty pick up. We're on at five."

Emily hung up the phone and poked her tongue out at Harvey, feeling about five. She hitched her mobile out of her pocket and called through to Crystal, walking to her room and closing the door against unwelcome eavesdroppers.

"It's my birthday, today," she announced when the medium answered. "How do you feel about going out to watch Greg and Pete splatter themselves all across the hall in a roller derby?"

WITH HER MUSCLES stiffening from their earlier exertion, Emily walked instead of driving to the shop, in the hope it would loosen her up again. Crystal tooted as she passed by, waving a hand out the side window.

"I didn't have time to get you a present," Crystal exclaimed as she clambered out of her car. "But I got you this."

Emily accepted the giant foam hand with a laugh. "It's perfect." She slipped it onto her right hand and waved the forefinger in a circle above her head.

"Be careful with that thing." Crystal primped her hair in the reflection from the charity shop window, then held the door open. "After you, birthday girl."

Walking past with a flounce, Emily gave a regal nod and pulled the foam hand off, airing out her fingers. She gave a normal-sized wave to Pete who was standing at the counter, in deep discussion with Greg. Out of habit, she crossed to the back of the store and looked up the staircase to the attic. To her surprise, a man was descending the steps.

"Oh," he said, putting a hand to his chest. "You gave me a fright."

"I have that effect on a lot of people."

It took Emily a second to decipher the man's words. He spoke with a strange, flat cadence, like someone hard of hearing. As he reached ground level, she recognised the features of Downs Syndrome and understood why.

"What were you doing upstairs?" Emily took a step back, so the man had room to pass by her. Instead, he stopped and stood in place, beaming a gigantic smile at her.

"The bathroom's on the ground floor," Pete called out, waving. "Go out through the rear door, not upstairs."

The man returned the wave and followed the directions while Emily crossed over to the counter to join Pete and Gregory. Crystal stared after the stranger for a second before coming over as well.

"That's Terrence Salem," Pete said with a nod to the corridor. "He's on the team."

"He's a roller-skater?" Crystal asked, her voice full of surprise.

"Best one we've got," Gregory said, a defensive note in his voice. "He can skate a lot quicker than me."

"And he doesn't care about getting hurt as much as I do," Pete added, "so he takes risks that would turn my blood cold."

"Sounds fabulous," Crystal said in a small voice, a frown of worry crossing her face.

"I don't know what Emily's been telling you about our team, but it's not as bad as it sounds." Pete shot Crystal a wink and draped his arm around Gregory's shoulders. "And we're about to break this one's cherry, tonight."

"Just so long as he doesn't break anything else," Emily

said, wrinkling her nose. "I want all the thrills and none of the spills, thank you very much."

Terrence joined them at the counter, raising his eyebrows as the conversation came to a natural end. "Pete tells me you used to work at an accounting firm just down the road from my old house."

"Did he?" Emily wasn't sure she liked people discussing her behind her back, but let it go. "What street were you on?"

"Gloucester. I lived in an apartment block close to the city. Ermine Villas."

Emily nodded her head, giving the man a more appraising look. "That's a nice spot. Pinetar must feel like a step down."

"Hey," Pete and Gregory called out in unison.

"I have family in Pinetar, so that makes a difference. Are we ready to go?"

"We're ready." Pete clapped him on the shoulder and turned to Emily. "Are you coming along with me, or with Greg?"

"With Greg," she replied, hooking her arm through the young man's elbow. "Since it's his big day."

"A little birdie told me it's your big day, too," Greg said, throwing an arm around Crystal's shoulders and leading the two women out to his dad's car. "Happy birthday."

The Roller Derby was taking place at the community hall in Pinetar Beach. Although referred to as an entirely different town by the locals, the beach was only forty minutes away from the main Pinetar township. On foot.

By car, it only took a few minutes before they pulled into the driveway.

"Should we wait for the others?" Emily asked as she struggled out of the backseat. She shook her legs out but, even after a minute, they still felt numb. To be on the safe side, she stayed close to Crystal as they walked towards the hall.

"I'm sure they won't get lost," Gregory said with a laugh. He waved to a couple of people filing into the building, roller skates looped over his shoulder. "And if they do, we've got spare skates. You can fill in for them."

"Although I'm happy to watch you break your neck," Crystal said, her expression aghast, "I've no desire to do the same. The last time I had a pair of skates on, they still played disco on commercial radio."

"I bet you were quite a mover, back in the day." Gregory performed a few quick steps and turned on his heel in a complete circle.

Crystal just rolled her eyes as they filed into the hall. There were two seats in the middle of the back row, offering the best view, and she claimed them with a toss of her jacket.

After a few minutes spent making small talk with people —most of whom Emily was just as surprised to see there as they were to see her—she sat and leaned her head back against the wall, closing her eyes.

"I think the main idea of being a spectator is keeping your peepers open," Crystal said with a giggle. "If you wanted a good night's sleep, I think you might be out of luck."

"It's been a long day," Emily said, stifling a yawn with the back of her hand. She cracked an eyelid open and watched her friend staring around the room with excitement. "You keep watch and tell me when the action is about to start."

It didn't take more than a few minutes before Crystal dug an elbow into her side. The skaters rolled out onto the track, their arms lazily hanging at their sides, in complete contrast to the speed they were travelling.

"Oh, I can't look," Crystal squealed, holding her hands over her eyes and peeping through her fingers.

"Wow!" Emily stared at the track, amazed at the grace and

determination of the men she worked beside every day. As the pace grew faster, she leaned forward, accidentally kicking her handbag onto the lower level.

"Thanks," she said as the woman on the seat below her handed it back. The zip was half undone and Emily checked the puzzle box was still in place, lifting it out briefly to admire its design.

Her eyes met with Terrence as he whizzed past on the track. His gaze stayed fixed on her as his body turned into the curve of the track. A split-second later he tumbled head over heels, the skaters behind him piling into a heap as they tripped over his prone form.

"I can't look!" Crystal shrieked again, staring at the growing carnage.

CHAPTER EIGHT

"Hey," Cynthia said the moment Emily woke the next morning. "Could you tell Wanda she has to teach me her tricks?"

"Didn't I tell you not to come into my bedroom while I'm sleeping?"

"You're awake."

"Only just. You were here waiting already."

Cynthia shrugged and batted the concern aside with her hand. "Never mind that now, I need to learn how to shoot stuff out of my hands." Her eyes gleamed. "Imagine the possibilities!"

"If she doesn't want to show you, I can't help." Emily sat up and groaned as her muscles reported the exact amount of over-exertion she'd subjected them to the day before.

"You could tell her you won't hunt down the spell book until she's taught me her secrets."

"I could but I won't." Emily shifted the covers back, feeling like a hot poker was stuck in every joint. "If what the sergeant said was right, we're living on borrowed time as it is."

"Didn't stop you going out last night." Cynthia sniffed and stuck her nose into the air.

"We couldn't do anything last night," Emily said, then wondered why she was bothering. "If you can't sweet talk Wanda into doing what you want, it's nothing to do with me."

A crash from the kitchen soon had her running, despite the protest from her muscles. Harvey offered an apologetic grin as he wiped pancake batter off the kitchen tiles. Peanut circled around his legs as he squatted, perhaps indicating where the blame should lie.

"Sorry if I woke you," he said. "I'm so clumsy these days, I tripped over my own feet."

"No worries. I was awake. I just hadn't bothered to get out of bed."

"Well, go get dressed and I'll mix up another batch," Harvey offered, rinsing the sponge out. "I make a mean pancake if I do say so myself."

Emily agreed, trying not to notice the new dishes piling up on the kitchen counter. Harvey had washed the ones from yesterday but left them stacked on the side to drain. Apparently, they'd been very wet because they were still there, waiting to be put away.

"I can see why his wife kicked him out," Cynthia said with an arched eyebrow. "Your brother is a bit of a slob."

"Get out," Emily whispered, wishing she could slam a door in the ghost's face. "I'm getting dressed."

"Nothing I haven't seen before."

"You're not making it any better."

"Fine." Cynthia tossed her hair from side to side, then floated out the door. She floated back in a few seconds later. "He's spilled flour all over the floor. Do you want me to poltergeist him out of here?"

"I want you to go into the lounge until I'm ready to face the day," Emily scolded.

"You mean, Harvey's bedroom? No thanks."

Emily tried to lift a t-shirt over her head but the protest from her arms overwhelmed her. It had been ages since she'd last done CPR and then only for practice. The real thing had used far more energy. Something she hadn't truly appreciated at the time, with adrenaline flooding her veins.

A pity she couldn't conjure up a new chemical rush—at least until she finished getting dressed.

"I can help you with that, you know." Cynthia wrinkled her nose. "If I can throw plates at a wall, getting a shirt over your head will be dead easy."

Emily had never wanted to turn down help more than she did right that second. Instead, she sighed and nodded. "Thank you."

"My mother always thought I'd grow up to be a nurse," Cynthia said as she arranged Emily's clothing. "I don't know why. Neither of us had a single caring bone in our bodies."

"You're cutting yourself short, there." Emily touched the back of her hairbrush, then decided the world would cope fine with her tangled curls. "You cared for Gregory for a long time."

"And Peanut," Cynthia added, cooing as the cat walked straight through the door.

This time, when Emily walked into the kitchen, Harvey was finishing up with a batch of crispy pancakes.

"Grab a plate and I'll load you up," he said, waving his spatula. "I picked some lemons to squeeze over top and there's sugar on the table."

It had been so long since Emily ate anywhere except on the sofa—usually with the television blaring—that to sit at the dining table felt novel. She squeezed out half a lemon and then scattered sugar over the top, letting the crystals absorb and dissolve in the juice.

The previous night, she'd arrived home late—for her, anyway—after accompanying the bruised team members to the twenty-four-hour surgery to have a doctor check over their injuries. Terrence had been the least affected, despite his position at the bottom of the pile.

After a late night stop for decaf coffee and cake, Emily had staggered through the door, exhausted. She'd raised a hand to her brother as she walked past but didn't allow herself to be pulled into a conversation.

In truth, she'd been disappointed to find him still awake. The back of her mind had held hopes he'd be asleep so she could sneak past him.

This morning, Emily didn't have any more conversation at hand than the night before. The only real question she had for her brother was 'how long are you staying?' and she didn't think that would receive a straight answer.

Their family had one thing in common—a high tolerance for avoiding any elephants in the room.

"That's better," Harvey said after a few mouthfuls. "Those biscuits didn't work out very well yesterday, unfortunately. Good to know I haven't lost all my skills."

"I didn't know you liked cooking," Emily said, sitting back and lacing her hands across her belly. The morning sun streamed in through the window, tracing a line of warmth across her back.

"Mum used to let me bake things as a treat," Harvey said, half-closing his eyes. "All I ever wanted to cook up was sweets and all she ever needed help with was our tea, so we compromised on biscuits and slices. You used to demolish my ginger crunch."

"That was yours?" Emily remembered the thick ginger icing and the snap of the crispy base. Nowadays, what bakeries called ginger crunch was actually a slice, no crunch to be had at all. She'd given up buying it in disgust a few years before her accident, never certain if her memory was playing tricks on her and it was simply a matter of her taste-buds maturing.

"I could make some while I'm here if you still fancy it."

"Yes, please," Emily said, so quickly that they both laughed. "What did you get up to yesterday?"

"After pulling your garage apart, I didn't do a lot. Most of the biscuits went in the bin, then I fell asleep on the couch while trying to decide what to watch on TV." He shook his head, a dreamy expression on his face. "The town looks exactly the same as I remember. Just a few chain stores instead of the old single-owner places."

Emily tilted her head to one side, remembering the row of old shops, each one named for the surname of the person who ran it. Or their parent or grandparent in cases where the business had been handed down the generations.

"Next thing you know, they'll be putting in the golden arches."

"I doubt it. You can see from the shape of the roof that the second-hand clothing store on Main Street used to be a KFC. Didn't work out for them."

"Thank goodness for small populations, eh?" Harvey gave her a wink, his favourite gesture from childhood. Emily couldn't do that or roll her tongue. No wonder they'd both been adopted for use in any situation by her brother. Sibling rivalry alive and well.

"I've got to follow up on a few things today," Emily said with a sigh, rotating her shoulders until they griped about even that small movement. "I'm trying to trace an item that sold at auction." She frowned. "At least, I think that's where it went."

Harvey bent forward, hiding his face as he gathered up

their dishes. "Can I take you out for a meal, tonight? I feel like I've barely seen you."

"You've been here less than a day," Emily pointed out, trying not to see the expression of disappointment on her brother's face. "But sure. Unless something terrible happens, you can shout me some fish and chips or something."

"Sounds good." Harvey's eyes brightened. "We can take them up to the beach and feed our leftovers to the seagulls."

"If we see any." Emily ducked her head down to hide a yawn. "They're getting scarcer every year."

"All the more reason to feed them the last of our chips, then."

THE AUCTION HOUSE might have been closed for the weekend, but the real estate agency was well and truly open for business. The short walk to the town centre loosened up Emily's shoulders enough for her to be able to raise her arms a short distance. Certainly, far enough to shake the realtor's hand when he greeted her at the door.

"Looking for a new place already?" Bryant Majors asked with a grin. He'd sold Emily her house when she moved to Pinetar.

"Not for me," she answered, then a listing caught her eye. "I wouldn't mind taking a flyer with me though. My brother might be in the market for something."

The small cottage listed appeared to be the same size as Emily's, but with an extra bedroom and located at Pinetar Beach. She'd avoided that end of town, not wanting to spend her days vacuuming up sand, but judging from Harvey's enthusiasm for eating there, he might not mind that particular effect.

"I can show you around the place this afternoon if you're

interested." Bryant jerked his chin at the leaflet. "You've missed the open home yesterday, but the owner spends most of his time back in Christchurch so I can take you around any time."

"I'll keep it in mind," Emily said with a nod, "but I'm actually after some information on a property rented through here."

"For your brother?"

Emily tussled with her conscience for a short second, then shook her head. "No," she admitted. "It's more for curiosity's sake."

"It's for a lot more than curiosity!" Wanda appeared out of thin air, indignation written over every inch of her face. "My sister's life is at stake."

"She can't tell him that," Cynthia retorted as she turned up on Emily's other side, arms folded, and her mouth set in a thin line. "If you're not going to teach me your magic at least do us the favour of using your head."

"The flat is here," Emily said, handing over her phone with the Street View image showing. "There's a middle-aged couple in it now, but it used to be occupied by two sisters."

"Oh, yes." Bryant sucked air through his teeth. "I remember that. Nasty business. Still, the landlord was within his rights to do what he did."

"What did he do?" Emily lost a short battle to keep a frown off her face.

"Well…" Bryant checked over Emily's shoulder, then gestured her further inside the office. "They had a year-long lease and had already given him notice they wouldn't renew when the accident happened."

"I suppose that's why it was re-let so quickly."

"That, and he had a great real estate agent."

Emily gave a giggle and waved at him to go on with his explanation.

"Since they'd given notice, the lease agreement said if they left any items in the house past the paid-up date, the landlord was entitled to put them into storage and pay for the facility using their bond."

"Okay." Emily pulled at her ear, staring at the ground in concentration as she worked out where Bryant was heading. "And when the bond money was used up?"

"Sold at auction." He gave a long sigh. "As I said, it's a nasty business. If that poor girl ever comes out of her coma, she'll be starting all over again."

"Did the landlord sell everything?"

Bryant shook his head. "Not him, the storage company. They had a few units with overdue fees and gave notice to the renters they'd sell off the contents to pay off the debt. I mean, I know it's within the letter of the law to send a notice to the last-known address but when everybody in town knows the recipient is comatose in a hospital bed, it doesn't sit right."

"Everything went to auction." Emily spoke the words as a statement, but Bryant nodded as though she'd put it to him as a question.

"Anything they can't sell there, probably just went straight to the dump."

Emily kept her gaze fixed on her shoes, not wanting to catch Wanda's eye. Despite the difficulty of recovering goods if they'd been sold, Emily preferred that option to trawling through a mountain of waste at the local tip.

"Let me know," Bryant said, tipping his head toward the flyer in Emily's hand again. "The owner is quite desperate to sell that bach, so I could get your brother a good price."

Just as Bryant said the words, a couple with two toddlers walked up to the window, browsing the selection of photos on display. Emily excused herself, escorting her two squabbling ghosts back home to fetch the car.

"Where are you going now?" Cynthia's voice sounded as though Emily had personally insulted her somehow.

"To the auction house."

"I thought it was closed."

"It is."

Still, she hoped there'd be somebody around to help out. If not, it gave her somewhere to sit and think without her brother hanging about.

Emily pulled into the car park but could see without walking up to the door that it was locked shut.

"Great idea," Cynthia said with her trademark sneer. "Anywhere else you want to go today? Perhaps a bank?"

Wanda spoke up. "My group home mother used to say, if you don't have anything nice to say, don't say anything at all."

"Words of wisdom." Cynthia gave her a pained expression. "The long winter evenings must've just flown by."

"Stop sniping at each other, will you? I need to think."

Emily turned the car around, just in time for another vehicle to pull into the otherwise empty lot. She waited for a minute, then stopped the car when she saw her helper from a few days ago getting out.

"We're not open," Sean said as Emily approached him with a wave. "You'll have to come back during the week."

"I don't have anything to sell," Emily called out, closing the distance. "But there was a question I wanted to ask."

The man gave a forlorn glance at the auction house door and Emily felt a pang of guilt. He'd probably just stopped by for a few minutes to make his job easier tomorrow. Now, here she was, taking advantage when he probably wasn't even being paid for his time.

"What d'you need?"

"Just information about some storage items." Emily pulled out the puzzle box and showed it to him. "Do you remember the lot this came in?"

"Sure." Sean put out a finger to touch the varnished wood. "I remember you taking a fancy to it. Was there some problem with the sale? I know you didn't win it in the bidding but payment's final, you know."

"No problem. I've just become aware there was a book that originally came along with this, but it wasn't in the box of goods I saw at the auction. I wondered if it'd been sold to someone else."

"Probably." He folded his arms. "You can't expect me to know what you're talking about from that description. We sell a lot of books."

She flicked a glance at Wanda, who nodded. "It's leather-bound with a golden chain to keep it secured. It also had fancy metal corners and there was a circular design embedded in the leather on the front."

Emily recited the information to Sean, who looked reluctantly tipped his head forward. "Yeah. I remember that one, but you're too late. It sold on Friday, too."

With a steadying hand on her stomach, Emily leaned forward, looking him straight in the eye. "It's very important that I track down the owner. Are you able to tell me who it sold to?"

"Of course, not." He took a step back, seemingly affronted. "That's against our policy and probably not something we could legally disclose."

"No. You have to tell us." Wanda tried to grab the man's arm, giving a frustrated huff as her hand sailed straight through his. "It's my sister's life on the line. Tell him!"

"Surely, it's not a secret? These are open auctions. If I'd seen the bidding, I'd know who'd won it."

"Yes." Sean smiled. "If you'd seen the auction, you'd definitely know who won."

Emily waited for a beat, but he didn't follow it up with anything further.

"Can't you do something?" Wanda turned to Cynthia, waving her arms. "Make him tell us. You can throw things about. Scare the life out of him until he tells us what we need to know."

"You know what that'll cost you," Cynthia stated flatly. "It's up to you."

"Please, can't you give me a hint." Emily let the exhaustion and excitement of the day before wash over her until a tear slipped out from beneath her lashes. "I'm not going to do anything bad with the information. I just really need to find that book."

Sean took another step back, fidgeting and throwing a longing glance towards the back door of the auction building. "I'm sorry," he said after a minute of silence. "I really can't tell you that the same man who originally won the bid on that item"—he jerked his chin toward the puzzle box —"also won the leather book you're after."

He strode away, not looking back. Emily was so surprised, he'd gone before she could thank him.

"What's happening?" Wanda asked. "Do you know what he meant?"

As Sean let himself into the back door, Emily turned to the ghost. "Yes. I know. Now, it's just a matter of finding him."

CHAPTER NINE

Cynthia leaned forward from the back seat, perching her chin somewhere above Emily's shoulder. "Let me see if I've got this straight," she said in a sing-song tone. "You're going to drive around town until you see the person you're looking for?"

"He's very distinctive." Emily jerked her arm as though Cynthia was a physical thing she could shake off. "I'm sure he'll stand out."

"Is he so distinctive he can be seen even when he's inside another car or a house?" She sighed. "You might want to think this through, Scarface."

Wanda threw a dirty look in Cynthia's direction. "Leave her alone. Unless you have a better idea, you're adding nothing to the conversation."

"My better idea would involve finding someone to give you a name, then getting his address from the white pages. Like a normal person."

Emily turned a corner, slowing as she saw a sign indicating children were around the place. The back alleyway on her right-hand side must lead through to the primary school.

Even though they wouldn't be around on a weekend, she still slowed the car down to a crawl.

"It's the first part of your plan I have a problem with," Emily said once her driving no longer needed her full attention. "Where are we meant to find this person who knows the name of the man we're looking for? Once you've got that sorted, try me again."

Wanda laughed in glee and pulled a face. Cynthia turned her attention to the passenger window.

"Hey," she said after a minute. "Isn't that one of Gregory's teammates?"

Emily glanced around, spying Terrence walking with slumped shoulders on the side of the road. She pulled up next to him, lowering the window as the car slowed and leaning over to call out through the passenger side, "Do you need a lift?"

The suspicious expression that resulted indicated Terrence had seen more than his fair share of 'stranger danger' lectures. He shifted from one foot to another while staring in the open window.

"It's Emily Curtis. I came to watch you skate yesterday, remember?"

Terrence nodded, a smile gradually dawning on his face. "Sure. Do you live nearby?"

Emily gave him her address but shrugged. "I'm not headed that way at the moment, so I can take you anywhere."

Terrence let himself be cajoled into the passenger seat, then buckled up securely. "I live down on Mapleton Terrace," he said. "The pink stone house with the dark green roof."

Emily remembered the street and found her way there soon enough. "By the way," she asked, trying to sound casual over the pounding of her heart, "do you know anyone around here with tattoos up their arm?" She turned into

Terrence's driveway, the neatly kept garden making her smile. "He has burn scars, as well."

"You mean Jake the Snake?" Terrence's face clouded over. "If I were you, I'd stay well away from that man. Every time I walk past his front lawn, he runs out and hurls abuse at me."

Emily coloured in reflected shame. "How dreadful! Believe me, I wouldn't be stopping by his place unless I needed to. Once our business is finished, I won't be hanging around a second longer."

When Terrence didn't offer the location, Emily prompted, "You'd be doing me a huge favour if you could tell me where he lived. My only plan was driving around until I spotted him."

She laughed, and Cynthia mocked her from the back seat. "I told you it was a dumb plan."

"He's on Alberton Lane. It's a dead end and his house is the last one on the right."

As Emily gave her thanks and waved goodbye, Cynthia let out a bark of laughter.

"What on earth are you doing, Witchy-Poo?"

Wanda flapped her hand. "I'm staying out of sight, what does it look like?"

Emily glanced behind her, giggling as she saw Wanda bent so low, she was half crouching in the footwell. "You remember you're a ghost? There's no one out here able to see you."

"You can see me."

"Scarface is special. I haven't found anyone else in town who can do what she does." Cynthia rolled her eyes. "Despite the claims of various mediums. Get up. You're making me nervous doing that!"

"I'll just stay put to keep safe."

"Who are you trying to avoid?" Emily eased the car back onto the road and spoke the address into her smartphone. A moment later Google Maps began to lecture her on the correct route to follow.

"I've met Terrence before and he's a lovely chap, but his elder sister is the Supreme."

Emily nearly slammed her foot on the brakes. "For your coven?"

"Yeah." Wanda risked a quick glance out the window, then breathed out a relieved sigh as the house receded out of view. "It's best I stay out of her way."

"Being dead is a good start," Cynthia said with a snort. "Or does your coven possess magic powers that let them see the dead?"

"If anyone could, it'd be the Supreme. Agnetha can probably hear me talking right now." Wanda didn't sound enthralled with the idea.

"If she's so powerful," Emily said, "won't she know a spell to free your sister?"

"She probably knows a spell all right, but she'd never use it to free Sheryl in a million years. Agnetha barely tolerates me but she hates my sister's guts."

Emily exchanged a glance with Cynthia, both of their eyebrows raised.

"What'd Sheryl do to hack off your dear leader?" Cynthia asked, her skin being thicker. She dropped her voice into a mocking whisper. "Did she steal Agnetha's man?"

"It's another of those things that's hazy and I don't care enough to find out, now." Wanda brushed herself down. "Isn't that the turnoff?"

The GPS on Emily's phone agreed, and she started to search for a house matching Terrence's description. It didn't take long to spot the one with rusting pieces of scrap metal, an overgrown lawn, and a roll of barbed wire topping the rotting wooden fence.

"Since this street's a dead end," Cynthia mused, "why

would Terrence be walking past this guy's front lawn, to begin with?"

EMILY'S THROAT was a desert as she knocked on the door. She cast a longing look back at the car, wishing she was safely inside it. Wishing she was anywhere except standing on the front stoop of a man who thought it was fun to throw insults at a man with Down's Syndrome. Or pound on her window when she bought an auction item out from under him, fair and square.

"Who're you?"

The call came from a window, the door remaining shut tight. Emily took a step back, then had to throw her arms out to both sides to steady herself as her shoe landed on a broom handle.

"Watch it! Some of that stuff's expensive."

Which is why you threw it on your lawn?

Emily bit her lip shut against the instant retort and regained her footing. "I'm here about an item I think you might have brought at auction," she said, her voice cracking. "It's an—"

"I know you!"

The window slammed shut and a second later footsteps pounded towards the door. When the young man threw it open, the pebbled glass shook in its frame.

"You're the one who stole the puzzle box. I've got the money." He dug into his back pocket, pulling out a tight curl of notes. "How much d'you want for it?"

Emily held up her hands. "No, I don't want to sell. I'm looking for another item. A book."

"Eh?" Jake tilted his head to one side, frowning at her as though she spoke a different language. "You want to swap?"

"No. I just want the book. It's important."

He looked over his shoulder, along the hallway. "I can't give you the book. It's the only way—"

Jake bit off the sentence, snapping his head around to face Emily. "Who sent you here? What do you know about a book?"

"Well, this is going great, Scarface. You have such a way with people."

Emily resisted the urge to cast a foul expression Cynthia's way and kept her gaze glued to Jake's face. There was something happening that she couldn't quite put her finger on.

"You do have the book, don't you?"

"Do you have the puzzle?"

They stared at each other for a tense moment, then Jake sighed and stepped back. His face was cast into the gloom of the unlit hallway. He shut the door.

Emily leapt forward and stuck her foot in the gap just before it closed. "Please, wait! It's vitally urgent I get hold of a book. It's leather-bound with a chain holding it closed. Do you have it?"

Jake put his eye up to the slit. "I'm not answering any of your questions until you answer mine. Who told you about the book?"

"Just let him know the truth," Cynthia urged. "What's he going to do? Shut the door in your face?"

"Please," Wanda begged, joining them on the step. "If we can't get the book, my sister might as well be dead."

"Wanda Hawthorne," Emily said, straightening her back against the anticipated ridicule. "It's a spell book to rejoin her sister's mind with her body and it's vitally important I get hold of it and perform the ritual soon, or Sheryl will die."

Jake stared at her through the thin gap, chewing on his bottom lip and scanning Emily from head to toe as though assessing her level of crazy.

"You'd better come in, then," he said finally, pulling the door open and stepping back to let her pass.

After the first flush of relief faded, Emily's nerves reasserted themselves. All the while she followed Jake through to the kitchen and sat in the chair indicated, her body began to beat a tattoo—*get out, get out.*

"How did you know Wanda?" Jake asked as he flipped the kettle on to boil. "Were you friends?"

"Not really." Emily flicked a glance at the ghost witch, then stared at her hands. "But it's a small town, isn't it?"

"You can say that again." Jake crossed to the cupboard and took down some cups, banging them onto the bench. "Every time I try to turn around, someone's in my business. You should hear the lies they tell about me, down at the pub."

"I can imagine." She raised her arm up to run her fingers through her hair, then groaned as the muscle spasmed, still not forgiving her for the day before. Emily coughed to disguise the sound. "I met somebody earlier today, said you chase him off whenever he walks by."

"Terrence Salem, right?" Jake gave a snort. "For some reason, his sister made it my business to ensure he doesn't get hurt around here. I like to keep a lot of spare parts out front and he always used to dig through them."

"To steal?" Emily felt horrified.

"Nah. He just likes to tinker with stuff. We've got that in common." Jake sniffed and spooned loose tealeaves into a pot. "You okay with black tea? I've got some chamomile in the cupboard if you prefer. Sheryl used to drink it."

"Black's fine." She chewed on a fingernail while sorting through what he'd just said. There were two juicy items to follow up on and Emily couldn't work out which to pursue first. "You knew Sheryl quite well, did you?"

"She's my girlfriend," Jake said simply, then shrugged. "Or was, I suppose is the right term now."

"I saw you visiting her in hospital," Emily admitted. "I wondered what you were doing there."

Jake smiled. It was amazing how the expression lifted him from the dangerous tattooed creep category and placed him into eligible bachelor land. "Didn't the town gossips fill you in on that bit, then?"

"No, they didn't." Emily returned his smile, finding it infectious. "I've a good mind to take them to task over it."

He laughed and poured out a cup of tea. "Milk?"

Emily nodded. "Why did Terrence's sister think he'd get hurt around here?"

Jake pulled up a chair, the wooden legs squeaking on the linoleum tiles. "I'm a bit of a packrat and sometimes the stuff I bring home just gets piled up a bit haphazardly. Terrence managed to pull on a car bumper and brought an avalanche of rusty metal down on his own head."

"Ouch."

"Nah, he wasn't hurt more than a scratch but his sister Agnetha had to take him down to the doctor's office to update his tetanus shot. Apparently, he doesn't like needles, and it turned into a big thing. She told me if she ever caught him 'round here again, she'd report me to the council."

"What business is it of theirs?"

"Exactly. But I don't need the hassle. I'm just trying to get by like everyone else. I asked Terrence to stay away, but the message didn't get through, so I yelled and chased him off the next time I saw him. That did the trick."

"Sounds like his sister shouldn't have put that burden on you in the first place," Emily said, feeling indignant on his behalf. "If she wants to protect him, it'd be a lot better to talk it through with him than place it on your shoulders."

Jake took a long sip of his tea. "Do you mind if I completely change the subject and ask if you've kept the puzzle box safe?"

"It's here," Emily said, patting her handbag. "Don't worry. Until it goes back in the body it's meant for, I'm not letting it out of my sight."

"I'm sorry if I gave you a scare at the auction."

Emily nodded. "You did, but it's understandable, considering what's at stake." She shifted on her seat. "How did you find out about the items?"

"Eavesdropping."

The guilty expression crossing Jake's face convinced Emily he was telling the truth.

"If you've hung around any members of the local coven for long, you'll know they keep their cards close to their chests. When I couldn't get any answers by asking directly, I tried a bit of stealth."

"In normal circumstances, I'd find that abhorrent," Emily began, and Jake took over from her.

"But these circumstances are anything but normal."

They laughed together, Emily still holding a part of herself back, so it was polite despite being genuine. "I don't want to hurry you, but if I could take a look at that book now, I'd be very grateful. I'm not sure how or where we're meant to perform the ceremony but just knowing we have the means to do it at all will ease my mind."

"Sure thing." Jake slid off his stool and put their mugs into the sink. "I put it up in the attic for safekeeping. You have to be a determined thief to steal anything from up there."

Although Emily shook her legs out, she couldn't lose the numbness. When Jake grabbed hold of the pull-down attic stairs, she declined to follow.

"Just a moment," he said, reaching the top. "It looks like the light's out."

"I've got a torch app on my cell if you need it."

Jake waggled his own phone. "Already ahead of you!"

He shone the bright LED in a semi-circle, frowning as he reversed the gesture.

"Is something wrong?" Emily called out, fighting to keep her voice steady despite the plunging fear in her belly.

"It's not here." Jake slammed his palm flat on the attic floor, causing a small cloud of dust motes to dance through the air. He breathed hard for a minute, then jumped off the stairs and flicked the lever to reverse them into their trapdoor. "I've been burgled. The book is gone."

CHAPTER TEN

"Is anything else missing?" Emily asked.

"Nothing I could see," Jake replied, running a tattooed hand through his hair until it stood up in spikes. He ran through into the kitchen and pulled open several drawers, clinking cutlery. "I've got valuables in here that haven't been touched. I can't believe this!"

"If the burglar only stole the book, then we can probably narrow down the list of potential suspects," Emily said, trying to make her voice soothing. "Who else would know what use it was? Who else cared enough about Sheryl to make it worth the risk to break in here?"

"The puzzle." Jake stared into her face with wild eyes for a second, then grabbed Emily's bag off her. While she gasped in protest, he rifled through the contents, closing his eyes in relief as he pulled the wooden box free. "I should probably put this somewhere safe."

"It's already somewhere safe," Emily protested, grabbing it out of his hand and taking back her handbag. "You're the one who wasn't able to hold on to your treasure. I think this is far better off staying with me."

He gave a reluctant nod, then groaned again and sat heavily on a kitchen chair. "I can't believe somebody broke in and found it without me even suspecting a thing."

"Do you want me to call the police?"

"No!" The vehemence of the response startled Emily and Jake seemed to notice, shaking his head in despair. "I mean, what would I tell them? The local station already has me on its radar because of a few innocent scuffles at the pub. They're not going to take me seriously when I say someone broke into my house to steal a book!"

"They might believe the two of us," Emily said, then flushed. Sometimes she found the police helpful. Sometimes they laughed in her face. Considering she'd been sitting in the station under arrest just the day before, she didn't rate her chances for the former.

"Would the book be of use to anybody except to rouse your girlfriend?" Emily glanced over to Wanda but the sick expression on the ghost's face made her feel even more dreadful and she returned her gaze to Jake.

"There're other spells in the book, sure. Nothing as urgent as this though."

"It came with a golden chain and engraved leather," Cynthia said, the calmest of the group. "I'm sure there are antiquarian booksellers who'd drool at the chance to just look at something like that."

"How old is the book?"

"Over a hundred years," Wanda said while Jake shook his head.

"Can you look up book dealers in the yellow pages?" Emily asked Jake, taking a seat beside him. "If there aren't any in town, we can probably rule that option off the list."

"It'll be Terrence," Jake said with an undercurrent of anger. "I just know it will."

"Doesn't his sister have a problem with Sheryl?"

"Agnetha has problems with everyone," Jake muttered, then gasped and moved to the window ledge. "There *is* something else missing. A decorated eggcup."

Emily moved to join him, seeing the circular smear of discolouration on the windowsill that indicated something had been moved. "Was it worth much?"

"It was porcelain and had some stones set into it." Jake shook his head for a moment, then moved into another room. "There's also a missing dining tray. It was sterling silver. And a greenstone statue."

"Perhaps we are looking at a petty thief, then." Emily didn't know whether to be upset or relieved. "If somebody broke in and was just taking a few odds and ends they could carry—"

"It doesn't make sense they'd go up in the attic."

Emily scrunched up her nose. "If the rope pull was hanging down, they might have had a quick look. Was it near the edge?"

"Yeah, I guess so." Jake appeared so miserable she had to turn away.

Cynthia pointed to Emily's wrist, and she frowned. "What time is it?"

"Just gone four o'clock."

Emily closed her eyes for a second. The day had got away from her completely. "I need to leave soon, I'm meeting someone for dinner. Why don't you make a list of everyone you can think of, and I'll meet you here tomorrow, bright and early?"

"But every second we leave it, they'll be getting further away!"

"Were you home all day, today?"

Jake hugged himself. "Yeah. I popped over the road to see Mr Harper for a few minutes earlier this morning, but he wasn't in."

"So if someone stole the book, they probably did it yesterday or Friday."

After a moment spent frowning, Jake reluctantly agreed. "Probably yesterday when I went to the hospital to visit Sheryl." His eyes filled with tears and he sniffed loudly.

"Then we're not going to lose anything by leaving it until tomorrow. We'll be able to find out a lot more from folks on a Monday morning than a Sunday evening."

"I suppose."

"Make up that list and I'm sure we'll get it sorted." Emily edged towards the front door, her stomach rumbling. She hadn't eaten since breakfast. "Set your alarm for six tomorrow morning, and I'll be here, ready to go, on the dot of six-thirty."

Without giving Jake a chance to talk her out of it, Emily scooted out the door.

"I FEEL like I should remember him, but my memory is all out of whack, except for the car accident." Wanda tapped her knuckles on the side of her head. "I'm sure it's all up here somewhere, I just can't get it out."

Emily, whose memory of her own car accident was almost completely excised, offered a sympathetic smile. "It's hard enough for people who survive to keep their memories going, I can't imagine what it's like when you died on top of everything else."

"Why don't you just magic up a spell to put it all back into place?" Cynthia sat on the edge of the bed, folding her arms. "Or isn't that in your repertoire?"

"I do have a vague recollection of him," Wanda continued, ignoring the other ghost. "Perhaps he was Sheryl's boyfriend, and I found the thought so disturbing, I blocked it out."

"He seemed fine to me," Emily said, wrestling with her T-shirt. Over Harvey's protestations that she didn't need to dress up to get fish 'n' chips, she was changing into a sundress and cardigan. Or trying to, at least. "The tattoos and scars are a bit frightening but once I got past that, Jake was a very nice young man."

"You need to think harder, Witchy-poo. If Jake isn't your sister's beau, then we don't want to follow up false leads. If he's lying to us about that, he could be lying about anything."

"I am thinking hard but it's not like we lived in each other's pockets. We shared a house, but I didn't keep tabs on Sheryl for every minute of the day. She used to go out all the time, overnight even, and not tell me where she was going. Apart from that, it's just all a bit hazy."

"Great. Hazy is all we need."

Emily clicked her tongue at Cynthia. "Leave her alone. It took you long enough to remember you were murdered, then you couldn't even think who'd done you in."

Cynthia's eyes narrowed. "I was hit on the back of the head."

"You still should have heard her coming."

Harvey knocked on the door. "Are you all right in there?"

Emily glared at Cynthia. "I'm fine. Just getting changed." She could hear him at the door, waiting, and bit down on her tongue. This was her house. She didn't owe anyone an explanation.

"Only..." There was a long pause. "Only, I heard voices."

Emily sighed and opened the door before retreating to the bed. "I talk to myself sometimes. Usually, there's no one else around to hear."

Harvey stared around the room, not meeting her gaze. "I do that, too."

"Was there anything else? Or are you calling the looney bin because I occasionally mutter to myself?"

"What's going on with your hand?"

With a start, Emily realised she was petting Peanut and stopped. "Nothing. It's just a muscle spasm. I get them since the accident."

Although he closed the door and walked back through to the lounge, Emily could tell her brother didn't believe a word.

EMILY WALKED up the stony beach with a wince. Although she remembered Pinetar Beach as being lovely to walk on, there was a couple of metres of pebbles to navigate before reaching the soft sand. Once she reached the bench where she'd left her shoes, she gave a happy sigh.

"Do you remember how Dad used to take out the Optimist sailboat, even though the Easterly always blew against it so hard, it could barely get away from the shore?"

"I remember him yelling at me when I jibed," Emily said, scrunching up her nose. "And for a while I thought 'you're luffing' was my nickname."

Harvey laughed, placing his hands on his hips while he stared out to sea. The froth of spume on top of the waves would deposit itself on the beach, only to be caught up and dragged back out by the next one. Even in the short time they'd been out there, eating their meal, the tide had crawled a good metre up the beach.

"When we had a school trip down here," Emily said, hooking her arm through Harvey's elbow. "I stood on the end of those concrete blocks until the tide came in. Gemma snapped a Polaroid of me walking on water and they published a copy in the paper."

"This town might not have been good for Mum or Dad, but it sure gave us some nice memories."

Emily frowned as she got in the car, happy to let Harvey drive. She couldn't think what he meant by his statement. As far as she knew, their parents had enjoyed the town. They'd stayed on when their children fled.

Her legs protested as Harvey parked the car in the driveway. She rubbed them, waving away her brother's offer of help. "It's just the muscles playing up. They'll come right in a moment."

Of course, one day they mightn't come right at all, but Emily didn't want to think about that now.

"Emily?" Harvey's voice sounded strained and her pulse skipped a beat. "Did you leave the front door unlocked?"

She closed her eyes and clutched her handbag to her chest. The hard shape of the puzzle box pressed its angles into her skin.

"Oh, no."

Feeling returned to her legs in a rush and Emily got out of the car and strode to the door. Harvey stood there, a hand over his mouth. He turned to her with eyes open wide with shock.

"We've been burgled."

CHAPTER ELEVEN

Déjà vu. Emily pushed past her brother to see the cabinets sitting open and the drawers not closed all the way. Unlike Jake's house, there'd be no attempt made here to cover up tracks.

"Don't touch anything," Emily warned, turning to see Harvey had his phone out.

"Police. We've been robbed."

She carried on through the rest of the house, unwilling to turn on the lights since the switches might hold fingerprints. Her stomach turned in a lazy spiral as she saw the covers on her bed messed up and the jewellery box open on her bedside table.

Emily didn't own anything other than costume pieces but the thought of someone going through her private things made her dizzy. The violation was too large to comprehend in one go—the knowledge washed over her in waves.

"The police said not to touch anything we think the burglars might have handled." Harvey stuck his head around the side of the door and looked around Emily's room. "I think they got in through the laundry window."

"Are they coming?"

"Yeah. The man I spoke to said they'll have a fingerprint expert come through tomorrow. He'll give you an incident report, which you can hand over to your insurance company to claim for anything missing."

"The police aren't coming down here now?" Emily frowned, certain she must have misunderstood.

But Harvey was shaking his head. "No. Since the intruder's gone, they won't be able to do anything. The sergeant also said to make a list of anything you know is missing, especially distinctive items so they can flag them with pawn shops and online vendors."

"Give me that phone." Emily snatched it out of Harvey's hand before he could pass it to her. She stared at the options in confusion. "Which one's redial?"

"Don't do that. I called 111 so they won't be very happy to hear from us again."

"Fine." She shoved the phone back. "I'm visiting the station, then."

Harvey stood very still. "Are you sure you should do that? Wouldn't it be better to let them deal with this in their own timeframe? They are the experts after all."

Emily stared at him for a long minute, her face a mask of concentration. "Is there something you want to tell me?"

"Eh?"

A crawling sensation spread over Emily's back and dug into her scalp. "You turn up on my doorstep, unannounced, needing a place to stay, and now my house is—" She gulped and waved her hand in circles. He could see exactly what her house was without her needing to speak.

"Are you asking me if I arranged someone to steal from you?" Harvey's lips were so pale they were almost blue. "Do I have that correct?"

She stared at her brother, feeling the gulf of years

between them. She didn't know this man, not really. Emily only knew the boy he'd sprouted from, and him not well.

"Yes, that's what I'm asking."

He shook his head, his gaze drifting to the floor while his arms folded tightly across his chest. "I didn't."

"Fine. I'm going down to the police station to give them a wake-up call. Are you okay staying here alone?"

Harvey nodded, still not meeting her gaze.

"I had to ask."

"No," he said in a soft voice. "No, you didn't."

EMILY TOOK the guilt she felt about doubting her brother and unleashed it as a tirade against Sergeant Winchester. "How dare you leave me and Harvey alone for the night, when someone's been through our house and stolen half our stuff? How can you call yourself a police officer when you can't even be bothered to lift a finger?"

"As I told your brother, there's nothing we can do tonight." The sergeant stood at the front desk, his eyebrows drawn so close together they formed one hairy line. "Until we have fingerprints to load onto the system, we've no way of tracking who might be responsible."

"What about the other evidence?" Emily smacked her hand on the counter. "There might be boot tracks at the window where the thieves broke in, or they might have left DNA on the drawer handles."

"All of which will wait until tomorrow."

"There's something else."

The sergeant raised his eyebrows and Emily gave a pointed glance at the constable nearest the counter. Winchester sighed and pushed away from the desk, walking out the back and into his office. She shuffled to catch up with him.

"What else is going on?"

"There's a ghost." Emily flicked her eyes towards the door then back again. Wanda stood there, cupping her elbows and with a pleading expression on her face.

"Unless your burglary is connected to—"

"It's Miss Hawthorne's sister." When he didn't respond, Emily prompted, "You know. From the hospital."

"You're talking to a coma patient?"

"No. The sister who died is with me. I think the thieves were after this." Emily pulled the puzzle out of her bag and placed it onto the desk. "I don't know if you're aware, but Wanda Hawthorne was a practising… Um… *Wiccan*. There's a spell book that's very valuable which is also connected to this item. It was stolen, probably yesterday."

"From you?"

"No." Emily clenched her hands together in her lap, thinking of Jake's insistence they leave the police out of it. Well, things had changed. "It was in the possession of a man called Jake. I'm not sure of his surname."

"Jake the snake." Sergeant Winchester gave a large sigh.

"You know him?"

"Oh, yes." He offered her a rueful smile. "Our station is very familiar with Jake's work."

"Anyway, he had the book stolen from his house and then this evening, someone's broken into my place. It can't just be a coincidence."

"And who do you think is responsible?"

Emily swallowed. Her throat was dry, and it took a few goes to clear the spittle in her mouth. She thought of Terrence at the roller derby, staring at the puzzle in her hand with such intensity he'd tripped, and knocked over half the players.

"Terrence Salem."

WANDA SHOOK her head as they stood outside the house. "I really don't want to go in there."

Sergeant Winchester stood at the doorway, talking to Agnetha and Terrence.

"Why don't you sneak in the back while we're speaking to them? I can't imagine it'll take long, but it might be good if you can find confirmation of the spell book being here."

The witch's face brightened at the thought. "Okay. If Agnetha sees me though..."

"Yeah." Cynthia gave a snort of laughter. "If she sees you, you're dead."

Wanda exchanged an amused glance with the other ghost. "That's right."

"Emily?"

She followed the sergeant's call and joined him on the step. Agnetha scanned her up and down, wrinkling her nose.

"My brother has been here all day," Agnetha said with a sniff. "We didn't even leave the house to go to the dairy."

"No, he hasn't." Emily's voice was so strong the sergeant took a step back. She shrugged, adding, "I gave him a lift earlier this afternoon."

"Where to?"

"Back here. I don't know where he'd been out to, but I picked him up closer to town and drove him here."

"And what?" Agnetha glared at Emily while Terrence shuffled from foot to foot behind her.

"I was out," he said. "But I've never stolen a thing in my life."

"Lying to the police isn't a great start, Ms Salem." Sergeant Winchester straightened his back and leaned forward. "I'll need to ask you and your brother some more questions. I'm sure in a few minutes, we can get this matter sorted out."

"Unless you have enough evidence to arrest my brother for this crime, we're not going to talk to you at all."

"Don't be silly, Agnetha." Terrence ducked around her side and pulled the door further open. "We're happy to answer some questions. I don't want this hanging over me tomorrow."

"Are you still working down at the butcher's?" the sergeant asked as he stepped past Agnetha, into the living room.

The sister's glare was so fiery, Emily half expected the officer to burst into flame. When he made it inside unscathed, she followed and took a seat.

"Now, if you could account for your whereabouts this afternoon and evening," Sergeant Winchester told Terrence, "that would clear things up nicely."

"I told you," Agnetha interrupted. "He was here."

"But you've already been proven a liar, haven't you?" The sergeant smiled sweetly. "And I'd prefer to hear everything from your brother directly."

"We did spend a lot of time here, this afternoon," Terrence said quickly as Agnetha opened her mouth again. "And I went to the burger bar around four, maybe four-thirty, to get our dinner. After that, we just sat inside, watching the telly."

"What programs?"

"None of your business," Agnetha snapped.

"We've been working our way through a box-set of DVDs —Crime and Lawlessness—and we saw a few episodes of that."

"Anything on live TV?"

"The weather?" Terrence glanced at Agnetha. "I don't pay

much attention when it's on, but my sister will be able to tell you what it said."

"And after that?"

"Back to the DVDs." Terrence flicked a hand toward the set in the corner where an image was paused onscreen. "Just a quiet night in."

"Who served you at the burger bar?"

"Wally." Terrence shrugged. "I don't know if he'll remember me. There were a bunch of teens hanging around outside with skateboards. He had his eyes on them the whole time he was serving me."

"Are you familiar with a woman name Sheryl Hawthorne?"

Terrence shot a glance at his sister, then nodded. "Yes. She's in the hospital, I believe."

"What about her sister?"

At that, the young man's expression turned to complete bafflement. "She's dead. Do you mean before that?"

"I was the guardian for both those girls when they were younger," Agnetha said and Emily recoiled in shock. The woman glanced over at her with an amused expression. "They were in care and no one would take the two of them on, because of their age. I fostered them through to the end of high school when they decided to go their own way. Since then, we'd fallen out of touch."

"Hard to fall out of touch in a town as small as Pinetar," the sergeant said with a deadpan voice. "People have to put in a lot of effort to achieve it."

Agnetha pulled a face. "I don't think any kid who grew up in that sort of environment wants a stranger telling them what to do, all of a sudden. They put up with me only for as long as they had to."

"Do you have possession of an old book?" Sergeant Winchester asked. He closed his notebook and slid the pen along the spine. "Engraved leather with a gold chain. Worth a lot in antiquarian circles, I imagine."

"We have books but none of them very fancy." Agnetha pointed to a small shelf in the corner. "I only download onto my Kindle, these days."

The sergeant stood and gave the books a cursory glance. "Right. Well, that'll be all from me tonight." He inclined his head towards Terrence. "If you could pop by the station sometime tomorrow, we'll grab a copy of your fingerprints. If they don't get a hit on the system, you're clear."

"But—" Emily jerked upright, hands wringing together. "Aren't you going to search the house?"

"Not without a warrant," Agnetha snarled at the same time Sergeant Winchester said, "No."

"But—" Emily repeated, still unable to follow up with another thought.

"Thanks for letting me in and answering my questions," the officer said, walking towards the front door. "I appreciate you being so generous with your time."

"It's always a pleasure to help out the law," Agnetha said in a generous tone, as though she hadn't tried to stop it happening ten minutes ago. "We're grateful for everything you do for our community, Sergeant Winchester."

Emily stumbled out the door, close on his heels, then whirled around as the door shut behind her. "You can't just leave it there."

"Yes, I can and that's exactly what I'm going to do." The sergeant opened the passenger side door and waved Emily inside the vehicle. "I'll drop you back home and someone will be around to your house tomorrow to check for prints."

Bested for the moment, Emily kept her lip buttoned as the officer dropped her home. Harvey was on the sofa, his eyes wrinkled so much from the effort of being closed, she knew he was faking being asleep.

Another shard of guilt at how she'd questioned him—no, accused him—earlier stabbed Emily in the chest and her eyes watered as she closed her bedroom door. She flicked on the overhead light, then blew out a huff of breath as she remembered about fingerprints. Too late, now.

Cynthia popped her head into the room, then left again with a small wave. Emily wished she could recreate her current expression at will if it had that benefit. She put her head into her hands, wanting to cry.

"Oh, my goodness," Wanda shrieked, hurtling inside and straight up to Emily. "You'll never guess what I found." Her eyes were wide, and her hair looked like she'd been tumble-dried.

"Well, if I'm not going to be able to guess, just tell me."

"There's a form on Agnetha's computer. It said that her application to withdraw life support has been submitted and is in the process of being approved."

"Pardon me?" Emily stared at the ghost in confusion, then a lightbulb went off in her head. "You mean, she wants to turn off your sister's machines?"

Wanda nodded, so upset that even Peanut noticed and batted at her legs to distract her. The witch bent over and picked him up, snuggling him against her chest and letting her ghost tears fall onto his grey fur.

"Agnetha has asked the courts for permission to kill Sheryl."

CHAPTER TWELVE

Pete's face said it all before he even opened his mouth. "How could you falsely accuse our teammate? As if that poor kid doesn't have enough strikes against him, you have to start dragging his name through the mud."

"I didn't do anything of the sort." Emily took a step back as Gregory joined Pete at the counter. Perhaps they'd been spending too much time together lately because their expressions were identical.

"Terrence works hard at the butcher," Gregory said, his voice soft but deadly. "With his disability, it took a while for him to find a suitable job. I'd have thought you'd be sympathetic, given your own struggles. He mightn't earn a fortune doing what he does, but he certainly isn't so hard up that he'd steal."

Although it had made perfect sense at the time, Emily had a sleepless night to second-guess her every decision. Already that morning, she'd had an earful from Jake. He'd woken to an enquiry from the police, prompted by her name-dropping.

He didn't want to chase up leads with her. If he found the book, Emily now wasn't even sure he'd share.

Of course, he will. It's not as though he can restore his girlfriend to life without your puzzle box.

Wanda stood at the counter, appearing just as unhappy as Emily's two coworkers but with even better reason. With her sister's life on the line more than ever, Emily couldn't afford to make mistakes.

"I'm sorry if I upset anybody but the police asked if I thought somebody might be responsible for the break-in and he was the only suspect I could think of."

Pete held his hands up to either side. "But why? You've only met him once and I don't think being a skater is any reason to think he'd steal."

"Somebody else suffered a burglary on the weekend and he thought Terrence was behind it."

Gregory took a step forward, his face twisting with anger. "Does your mystery victim have a name?"

"He does but not one I'm telling you, given your current mood." Emily folded her arms. "I've said, I'm sorry. There's nothing else I can do. I can't rewind time and take it back."

"Leave them," Wanda said. "If they want to prance around being upset over their friend, they'll be no good to us."

Emily shot her a glance but before she could refute the suggestion, Pete was echoing the idea.

"Perhaps it's best if you leave it to Gregory and me today. We can sort through everything from the weekend and having the extra work might help give us time to cool off."

Although she agreed, as Emily left the store, she had to fight back tears. Jake didn't want her assistance any longer, Harvey was sitting at home resenting her, and now she couldn't even busy herself with work.

"Don't do that," Cynthia said, falling in beside Emily.

"Do what?"

"Start dwelling in self-pity-land. If your coworkers are giving you the day free to do what you want, then use it wisely. It's not as though you need help to research a crime. You did pretty well sorting out my little mess."

"We should follow up on the court order," Wanda said, Cynthia's words seeming to clear the confusion from her brow. "If we can put a stop to that, it buys Sheryl more time."

"I used to know some lawyers back in Christchurch, but they were all involved in financial law. I could try them, but it might just lead us around in circles."

"Better that than not try them and find out later they could've helped."

Cynthia sounded so perky, Emily shot her a glance weighted with suspicion. The ghost's face was perfectly innocent—another reason to suspect she was up to no good.

Still, if she wanted to appear helpful, Emily should take advantage. She pressed the green button on her phone to bring up her old contact list, then displayed it to Cynthia. "Could you point out the ones tagged with lawyer?"

Once she'd selected five cards from the three dozen or more loaded, Emily composed an email aloud to her phone. When she'd been a child, talking into your hand would earn a person more than a few curious glances. These days, it had become so commonplace that none of the passing pedestrians stared.

"Until they reply, should we try to eliminate the obvious?" Emily said to her companions. "I'd rather use the computer to hunt down possible booksellers with an interest. Once they're ruled out, we can try to weasel some information out of the sergeant or one of the constables."

Wanda snorted. With Cynthia on her best behaviour, it now appeared they were swapping roles. "Given his expression at the house last night, I don't think that'll work."

"It definitely won't if I don't give it a try."

As Emily walked up to her front door, her hands were shaking. She'd escaped the house without talking to Harvey and wondered if it was worth hoping he'd made himself scarce for the day.

"You're back early."

Nope. She gave him a sideways glance and decided her brother didn't appear too unhappy. "The others are going to handle things today between them." When a frown started to crease Harvey's brow, she hurried to add, "They thought it best I recover from the shock of the break-in last night."

Not that her coworkers had expressed any concern about that. Emily had to console herself with the thought that if she hadn't forced the sergeant around to Terrence's house to interrogate him, they would have lavished sympathy upon her.

"I'm really sorry about yesterday," she said, her voice nearly disappearing. "I had no right to ask you those questions."

"If it'd been my place, I'd have been upset, too." Harvey wiped his hands on the tea towel and Emily realised the bench was clear for the first time since he'd arrived. "When you're in shock, sometimes things don't come out the way they should."

His empathy made Emily feel even more of a heel than she had been. "Thank you for that," she said. "I don't deserve your generosity."

"You're the one being generous, letting me crash here until I get back on my feet."

Emily was halfway to her room before she understood her brother's current explanation contradicted what he'd told her this far. Still... She shrugged and closed the door softly behind her. Harvey staying with her was a problem she could resolve later.

None of the lawyers had emailed back but Emily guessed her early Monday morning message would be buried at the bottom of a large weekend avalanche. She asked her laptop to search for second-hand booksellers, then listened to the results.

She knew one of the shops but wouldn't have classed it as a bookseller. By straining her memory, Emily vaguely recalled the furniture shop had a tiny section with volumes displayed on the shelves. If Google hadn't just informed her to the better, she would have sworn they were just for decoration.

One place sounded more likely, right until it got up to the section about specialising in military history. Another sold books but Emily knew the shop and wiped it off the list—a remainders table in front didn't really count.

"What are you doing?" Wanda sounded anxious and Emily gave her a curious glance. She supposed if the situations were reversed, she'd be lost in worry over her sister. "We should at least pay these places a visit. Any of them could've been the ones to break into Jake's place. You can't just cross them off the list without checking."

"What do you think a visit's going to do?" Cynthia didn't sound as snide as usual, but Emily could sense the compulsion laying under the surface. "It's not as though they'll have a stolen book out on display. If any of them really did steal the spells, it's far more likely to be on order for a private sale."

"You don't know that. The people around this place are sometimes as thick as two planks." Wanda's face flushed, a spot of colour high on each cheek. "Don't lecture me on what they would or wouldn't do."

Emily tried to intercede. "Nobody's lecturing—"

"I'm just laying all the cards out. If there's a place in town which deals in high-priced books by appointment, sure. We've nothing to lose following it up. But a shop selling furniture with someone trying to offload a few second-hand books on the side isn't going to have it."

"You don't know. You're not the expert."

"I'm better schooled than you."

"Ha! While you were spending time getting your nails done, some of us were living in the real world."

"The real world? Playing at being witches in the middle of the forest? Give me a break. You wouldn't know the real world if it came up and bit you on your big nose!"

"You're the one who wants to know the secret behind my powers." Wanda placed her hands on her hips and tilted up her chin. "You've been begging me for days so don't think I don't know what you're really after."

Emily put a hand up to her forehead. A migraine was spiking into her temple, leaving her vision pulsing in a colourful wavy line. "Could you both please be—"

"I just wanted to see if it was a trick." Cynthia flapped her hand in a dismissive gesture. "If someone as base as you can do it, I don't think—"

"Base? You're the one who loads on their makeup with a trowel."

"At least I've got something worth putting it on. With features like yours, it's no wonder you never—"

Emily's temper snapped, and she yelled, "Both of you be quiet!"

The two ghosts stared at her, their eyes wide in surprise.

Too late, Emily remembered she wasn't the only living human in the house. Footsteps pounded and Harvey wrenched her door open. "What's going on in here?"

Between her flare of anger and the thumping in her head, Emily couldn't think of a lie. "I was talking to the ghosts."

Harvey frowned. "You can see spirits?"

Emily was so frozen at what had just happened, she could barely nod her head.

Then her brother shocked her to the core.

"You mean, like Dad?"

CHAPTER THIRTEEN

"Are they still here, right now?" Harvey glanced around the room before directing his attention back to Emily. "It's a bit creepy, isn't it?"

"They're with us." She rubbed her temple where her headache still beat with a fierce rhythm. "Sitting here isn't so bad. It's when I wake up in the middle of the night to find them staring at me while I'm sleeping that freaks me out."

"Ugh." Her brother shuddered. "Do they really do that?"

"Far too often for my liking," Emily said, enunciating every word while looking straight at Cynthia. "No matter how often I ask them not to."

She reached out and pulled Peanut into her lap, the strokes along his fur soothing her as much as the cat. "I don't remember Dad seeing spirits. When did that happen?"

"All the time." Harvey tipped his head to one side, staring up into the corner. "I think Mum tried to shield us quite a lot. Back then, the town wasn't quite so welcoming as it is now."

Emily snorted. "You think this is welcoming?"

He flapped his hand. "Your friend's a medium and we

passed a wizard for hire sign out on the road to Pinetar Beach." He wrinkled his nose. "I even saw a person advertising a yoga class for dogs. You might still get a bit of attention but believe me, it's nothing like what Dad suffered through."

"I don't remember it at all." Emily picked at the dry skin on her top lip. "Had he stopped before I was old enough to notice?"

"He never stopped." Harvey frowned and traced a figure-eight on the wooden table-top. "Do you remember Mr Childers? From down the road?"

"Sure." Emily gave her brother a sharp look. "He wasn't a ghost."

Harvey laughed. "No, but he needed help to get rid of one. Dad spent every day for a month down at his place, working throughout the night trying to work out what would send the spirit on its way."

She rubbed at the tender spots beside Peanut's ears, earning herself the echo of a purr. "I think I can recall when Dad stayed away for a long time." She shrugged. "If I noticed, I probably thought he and Mum were having troubles."

"It was about the same time as your friend Tiffany's parents split up," Harvey said, nodding. "That makes sense. But what about Gwendolyn Pallweaver? She woke the entire house up screaming one night."

"Mad Gwen?"

"Is that what you called her?"

Emily pulled a face. "It's what everyone in my class called her. Are you saying Dad was mixed up with her?"

"She was nutty beforehand but yeah, he helped her out. There were lots of cases over the years. Sometimes people came knocking, wanting a hand with a restless spirit and Dad couldn't see them to help."

"Oh, yes." Emily eagerly nodded. "I find that too. If they

appear, they stick around until they've worn out their welcome but if I can't see them from the get-go, I never can."

"Dad used to reckon they were just trying to get attention, you know?"

"Crystal says much the same."

"Is she your medium friend?"

"Yeah. We were going to make a business out of it when I discovered I could first see the ghosts, but apart from one or two, I can't see what's haunting her clients at all."

"Still, it's nice you have a friend with the same gift."

Cynthia burst out laughing, and Emily put a hand to her face to hide a smile. "It's nice to have a friend but I don't think we share anything."

"Are you saying she's a charlatan?"

Emily rubbed her fingers along her scar. Whenever her head was aching, the twisted tissue picked up the same beat. "I'm saying Crystal helps people who aren't haunted with their spirits, and I help people who are with theirs."

"It's a pity Dad hasn't turned up to haunt you," Harvey said with a quick smile. "He could pass on all the tricks of the trade."

"I guess it means there was nothing holding him back. At least we can rest assured, he and Mum weren't murdered."

"Is that what your current ghost is trying to sort out? A murder?"

"No. That would be too easy." Emily pulled Peanut close and gave him a tiny kiss on the top of his head before releasing him. "Do you believe in witches?"

"In Christchurch or Wellington? No. Here? Sure."

Emily wondered if there was a mystic code she should have sworn an oath upon. Something to stop her spilling the spirit's secrets. Too late, if there was.

"Wanda Hawthorne was a witch, and she put her sister's

soul into a puzzle box to save her. If we can't find the spell to release her soon, then she'll die."

The corners of Harvey's lips curled for a second, then his face grew serious. "Okay. Is that what they took from the house last night?"

"No." Emily pulled out the wooden toy. "This is what they were after, so they weren't successful. Unfortunately, the same person—or people—had also burgled the place where the spell book was being stored."

"And they were successful at that burglary?"

"Yeah. They were."

Harvey linked his fingers behind his head and leaned back, letting his eyes gaze up at the ceiling. "Was anything else taken?"

"From here or from Jake's?"

His gaze shot to Emily's face. "Jake the snake?"

She shifted on her chair, suddenly uneasy. "Yes. He used to date Wanda's sister, and he's trying to restore her, too. Why? What do you know about him?"

"There're a few people in town I've kept in touch with over the years. I've heard a few tales here and there."

Harvey scratched at the stubble on his chin. Only a few hours past shaving and it was already deepening into shadow. Emily might have missed out on her Dad's gift, but she remembered enough to know he'd been the same.

"If there were other things stolen from Jake's place, it might be nothing to do with your quest."

Emily smiled at the word. It was so reminiscent of fantasy and adventure it fit her current situation quite well.

"There were a few items missing. Silver, mainly."

Harvey rapped his knuckles on the wooden table. "Then I might have a contact who can help us out. How do you feel about spending your morning down at the tavern?"

"It will feel as though I've strayed completely off the right path." Emily gave her brother a broad smile. "Let's go!"

WITH A RASPBERRY COLA IN HAND, Emily perched next to Harvey on a stool at the bar, struggling to balance. Even without the encroaching numbness in her leg muscles, she'd never been great with barstools. If she had her wish, every chair in the world would be built with a solid back.

"If we're sitting along here, how are you going to question anybody?" she asked, giving the tavern a quick scan.

"Don't worry. The person I'm searching for hasn't arrived, yet. He's probably out the back doing some trade."

Her watch announced it was ten o'clock, the robotic female voice sounding as out-of-place as Emily felt. She pressed the button on the side three times, condemning it to silence while her brother gave her a long stare.

"How hard do you find it, just getting through a normal day?"

She shrugged and took a sip of her drink. The old treat from her childhood had lost none of the thrill in her transformation to an adult, one of the few things that had stayed the same. "I get by just fine. There's plenty who have worse to deal with."

"I thought you'd be better off by now." Harvey took a long swallow from his pint glass, a mild lager in a warm shade of amber.

The condensation beading on the glass made Emily shiver. With the days creeping farther into Autumn, a cold drink wasn't the welcome sight it would have been a few months ago.

She chewed her bottom lip, warring between the truth or

an easy lie. "I'm not going to get any better. In fact, the doctors have warned me I'm likely to deteriorate."

Harvey frowned and ran a finger up the side of his glass, flicking the drop onto the stained oak bench. "You didn't tell me that."

"I didn't know that until a few months ago. It came as a nasty surprise."

"Is that why your limp gets worse during the day?"

Emily swallowed hard, taken aback that he'd noticed. "There're some bone fragments left in my head from the accident. They're pressing on the wrong bits of my brain but it's too dangerous to operate and get them out."

"Oh, sis. Why didn't you say something earlier?" Harvey turned away from her, his voice catching. "I could've been here for you."

"You know me." Emily stared down into the dark red of her drink. For a split second, it looked like blood and oil, then she blinked, and it turned back into a harmless soda. "I always prefer to deal with things on my own."

"That's the problem. I don't know you." Harvey pulled a handkerchief out of his pocket and wiped his nose.

The old-fashioned affectation tugged the corners of Emily's mouth up into a smile. Heaven forbid he upgraded to tissues.

"We haven't spent time together since we were little and now, I have no idea how to talk to you about anything serious."

Emily waved her hand around the bar. "These are serious matters." When her brother's brow darkened, she added, "You're doing just fine."

"I know you don't want me here but—"

Harvey broke off and his gaze followed a man who'd come into the bar from a side door. His almost-empty pint glass banged down on the counter and he rose, not even glancing at Emily. "I'll just be a minute."

"If that's your contact, I should come with you."

"Once I have a word."

Harvey walked away before Emily could raise another protest. He raised a finger to the man, and there was an exchange of jerked chins and raised shoulders until the pair sat at a corner table.

"Can I get you another one of those?" the bartender asked, and Emily stared in surprise at her empty glass.

"Yes, please."

She tried to keep tabs on Harvey from the corner of her eyes, but it was hard. When she saw him throw back his head and laugh, her stomach tightened into a cold, hard ball.

Finally, after a good ten minutes of intense chat, Harvey signalled for Emily to come over. She struggled off the stool and weaved her way through the tables and chairs to reach them.

"You're looking for an old book, I hear."

Emily nodded at the man. He had straggly hair and a complexion that spoke of too little sun and too much drinking. A starburst of burst capillaries lit his nose up like Santa's favourite reindeer.

"I've fielded enquiries about it before. For a long time, nobody seemed to know where it was or who had it." The man leaned back, squinting at Emily through deep-set green eyes. "Then the title suddenly came up for auction."

"That's the one." The knot in Emily's stomach loosened. At least they were on the same page. "Do you know—"

Harvey winced, and the man held a hand up to cut her off. "I've already heard enough on the subject from your brother. I can tell you the queries came from four different sources."

He took a sip from his pint and looked at the low level with a disappointed expression.

"Can I get you another?" Emily asked, reaching for her bag.

"I'll get us a round in," Harvey said, escaping for the bar.

Emily thought for a few minutes the man wasn't going to continue until her brother returned, then he coughed and sat forward. "One of the men originally asking questions was the same man now claiming the book's been stolen."

She raised an eyebrow but didn't feel any real sense of surprise. "Jake doesn't have it, anymore. I'm sure of that."

"No."

She desperately wanted to ask questions, to move this molasses-textured conversation along, but Emily bit her lip and turned to watch her brother's progress. Even though she had a full glass in front of her, Harvey had ordered a refill. He grabbed the two pints in one hand and frowned as they tipped.

"There was an old lady asking." The red-nosed man looked Emily up and down, then amended, "A middle-aged lady."

"Younger than me?"

"Yeah. She was cagey about the whole thing, but I knew what she wanted." He snorted at a memory. "The woman wasn't nearly so subtle as she thought. When she opened her Louis Vuitton bag, a bundle of cash came spilling out. She was so ready and willing to pay, I felt bad not being able to take the money off her."

The man paused, tipping his head to one side. "Well, not *much* money, anyway. I promised to keep her informed and charged a fee for it. That's just common sense."

"Who else?"

"Some bloke with Down's Syndrome."

Emily jerked back, nodding. "Terrence Salem." As the

man stared at her across the table, Emily frowned. "The police already questioned him."

"The police." He flicked a hand up as though brushing away an annoying fly. "They wouldn't know what's really going on if you sat down and explained it in minute detail. He's been asking, too."

"Why?" The question escaped from Emily's mouth before she could think to stop it.

"You don't stay in my line of business long asking why." The man gave a tight smile. "I also got asked a bunch of times by a red-haired kid. A girl just out of her teens. She was obviously working for someone else, but I don't know whether that someone was one of the aforementioned, or a separate buyer who wanted to keep themselves right out of the frame."

Harvey appeared back, loading up the table with the drinks. The man took his new pint and drained it in one long chug. He sighed in pleasure as he banged the empty glass down. "That'll do me."

It wasn't until her brother tugged on Emily's arm that she realised the man wasn't talking about the beer—he was talking about their conversation.

"Did you get what you needed?" Harvey asked as they abandoned their drinks at the table and hurried outside the pub.

"I think so." Emily cast one last glance back at the tavern, the strange man silhouetted against the corner window. "At least now I have an idea where to start looking."

CHAPTER FOURTEEN

"Okay," Emily said, sitting across from Crystal. "Since your next appointment's still twenty minutes away, I hoped you might recognise a few folks in town just from their descriptions."

It was a good bet. Crystal might not have a gift for communicating with the dead, but she was an excellent source of information about the living. Her floofy hair hid a mind like a steel trap. Not only did she regularly converse with a wide cross-section of Pinetar's population, her brain stored up every tidbit of gossip anyone had ever said to her.

Crystal shifted on her seat and linked her hands across her belly. "Shoot."

"Do you know a red-headed teenager?"

"Girl or boy?"

"Girl."

Crystal scrunched her eyes and stared up at the ceiling. "I reckon that'll be Belinda Bierswack. She's a real ginger. If not her, I've got the names of a couple of strawberry blonds who might fit the description in a pinch."

"Is she still in school?"

A joyous laugh greeted that question. "Belinda wasn't even in school when she should've been. As soon as she could legally sign out, she's never looked back." Crystal frowned and shifted so her elbows rested on the table. "I think she had a job at the clothing store on Banks Lane. The one with the price tags which'd make your eyes water."

"Really?" Emily chewed her lip. "I'm not sure that fits with a burglar."

"Oh, she'd be up for that, all right." Crystal snorted and wrinkled her nose in amusement. "Belinda's never been one for the straight and narrow. I keep expecting to find out she's filched a wallet while a customer's in the changing rooms or something. Give it time."

"Have you had many dealings with Terrence Salem?"

"The man from the roller derby?" When Emily nodded, Crystal put a finger up to her cheek. "I've heard a few things about him on the grapevine. This time last year, he was in a bunch of strife."

"What sort of trouble?"

"He got mixed up with a biker gang. They used him for moving drugs around the place." Crystal shrugged. "Because who's going to question a kid with Down's Syndrome. Not that he's a kid, anymore."

"How old is he?"

"Early thirties. Agnetha must've read him the riot act because once he got disentangled from the gang, he got himself a real job and there's never been a peep of trouble from him again."

Emily placed her hands flat on the table, eyes half closed as she concentrated. "I didn't realise he was as old as that."

"No. He still looks a lot younger than he is." Crystal's fingers leapt up to her face to explore the crow's feet extending out around her eyes. "I wish I had that trouble."

"How old is Agnetha?" Emily asked, then remembered

what the sergeant had said about her becoming guardian to Wanda and Sheryl. "Is she really his sister or is he a foster kid?"

"They're brother and sister, all right. She'd have maybe twelve years on him. The parents thought they were done with all that, then Terrence came along as a surprise."

"Where are the parents?"

"Auckland. The Mum's some bigwig with the university up there. They started off in Christchurch, Agnetha moved out here, then Terrence followed after his run-in with the gang."

Emily sat still for a moment, shuffling people around in her head to fit the new descriptions.

"Do you know anyone in town with a penchant for Louis Vuitton?"

Crystal glanced at her sideways. "Agnetha again. What's all this in aid of?"

"Harvey introduced me to someone at the pub. A fence. He gave me a few descriptions of people who're after the same book I'm looking for."

"If it's your witch-ghost, that makes sense. There've always been rumours around town Agnetha is tied up with some sort of modern-day coven."

Hoping she wasn't telling tales out of school, Emily said, "She's the Supreme."

"Well, she'll be your best bet, then. If there's a spell you need help with..."

"Apparently, she wasn't overly fond of Wanda and she hated Sheryl. I don't think I'm going to find any help there."

Crystal barked out a laugh. "Well, if she's not going to volunteer to help, what are you going to do? Even if she has got her hands on the spell book that you're after, I'm fairly sure it'll be the worst idea to steal it back."

"Considering that we're running out of time, even a

terrible idea is better than none." Emily ran a hand through her hair, still feeling the CPR exercise from the other day in her tired muscles. "But if she has taken it, I don't where it's hidden. Wanda had a look through the house while the police were questioning her and—"

"You took the police to Agnetha's house?" Crystal's mouth fell open with shock. "Man, I wouldn't want to be in your shoes."

"Nobody in their right mind would ever trade them," Emily said with a grin. "And that's without me taunting the lead witch around the area."

"Well, if you do need help…"

"You'll be my first phone call. I'll give Belinda a try but it's looking more and more likely Agnetha or her brother are the ones behind the theft."

"In that case, I'll write a lovely speech for your funeral," Crystal said, laughing as she escorted Emily out of her front room.

EMILY AVOIDED the price tags as she pretended to browse the dresses inside 'Festivals and Frolics.' She didn't want the expensive items to distract her attention and make her clumsy. It was hard enough to snatch a few casual glances at Belinda without fear of damaging a dress she'd have been lucky to afford in her old job.

"Can I help you?" the owner asked, sidling up to Emily. Maybe a sixth sense was kicking in because the woman gave her a long, appraising stare.

"I'm just looking," Emily said with a polite smile. "I'm not sure anything here takes my fancy."

"Were you shopping for a special occasion?"

"A wedding." The lie slipped from Emily's tongue with

such ease she felt rather proud. "It's my niece, and I'd really appreciate a younger person's opinion." She felt a bit guilty for using the same made-up relative for the second time in as many weeks.

The owner's smile didn't even falter as she turned and beckoned Belinda over to their side. "Maybe Bel can help you out, then. Is she about your niece's age?"

"A bit younger, perhaps." Emily pulled out a lime frock with large white flowers dotted at random over the fabric and held it up to her neck, smiling at the young redhead. "What do you think?"

"It'd be great for a funeral," the woman scoffed, nudging aside the proprietor to take another dress off the rack. "This should be more appropriate."

The garish sun-frock was festooned with orange and yellow slashes on a background of bright red darkening to deep maroon. Emily did her best not to wince as she took the garment out of Belinda's hands. "Do you really think this suits me?"

"Try it on." The young woman led Emily to a pair of changing rooms out the back. "You'll see."

"Do you mind staying here?" Emily asked quickly as it looked like Belinda was about to head back to the main shop. "Only I get claustrophobic and it helps if there's someone outside to talk to."

The woman stared at her with a disbelieving expression but stayed. "Sure. Whatever."

"Thanks." Emily pulled the curtain across and struggled to pull her T-shirt up over her head. "Have you worked here long?"

"A few months," the bored reply came. "It's really great."

The deadpan delivery made Emily smile. "Are you interested in clothing or design?"

"Not really. I like denim and leather."

Emily lost focus for a few seconds as she manoeuvred into the dress. For a horrifying second, she thought her arm had managed to tear a hole, but it was just the movement of a crossover flap held in place with Velcro.

She surveyed her reflection in the small mirror, then pulled back the curtain to examine her full-length reflection in the one outside. The garish colours caused her rosy complexion to deepen into a flush, like a practising drunkard or a woman whose blood pressure was off the charts. The placement of a yellow streak near the neckline threw a jaundiced pallor onto her chest and chin.

With a turn one way, then another, Emily kept her horror to herself. "What d'you think?"

"It's great," Belinda answered in the same dull monotone. "Really suits you."

"It makes me look a hundred years old," Emily snapped, clicking her fingers to draw the young woman's attention. "Rather like a book I heard you had an interest in."

"What?"

The girl stepped back but Emily matched her, holding up an accusing finger to point at Belinda's chest. "I talked to a fence at the tavern and he said you'd been asking about a spell book that belongs to me. It was stolen from a dear friend's house. You know anything about that?"

The young woman's eyes opened wide, and she jerked her head around. Emily didn't care if it was to check the owner couldn't hear or to seek help, she grabbed Belinda's chin and forced her head back to face her.

"Don't pretend you don't know what I'm talking about. Who're you working for?"

Belinda brushed Emily's hand away, her face twisting into a snarl. "You're talking nonsense," she said in a furious whisper.

For a second, she didn't know what to do. Then she

smiled broadly at the girl. "What did you say to me?" she asked in a high, shocked voice. "Didn't your manager teach you to treat customers with respect?"

The redhead's eyes opened so wide the whites formed a complete ring around her irises. Her mouth opened and closed like a gasping fish.

"Tell me the truth," Emily whispered, stepping closer. "Or you'll end the day searching for another job."

"Agnetha Salem," Belinda spat out. "That's who you're looking for."

"Oh, sorry," Emily said in a louder voice, accompanied by a tinkling laugh. "My mistake. At my age, I'm always hearing things wrong. I'm a nightmare to watch TV with, I can tell you."

She snapped the curtain closed, struggling back into her normal clothing and leaving the shocking dress in a strident heap of colour on the floor.

"Thanks for all your help," Emily said as she shooed Belinda back into the main shop. "But I think I might consider a few other options before committing."

With a mincing wave to the shop owner, she stepped outside.

It appeared all roads led back to Terrence and Agnetha. Wanda might not have been able to find the spell book in their house the night before, but Emily thought it was time to take another look.

CHAPTER FIFTEEN

As Emily was heading inside, her phone rang. A photograph of an old lawyer buddy popped up onto the screen and she smiled. It had been a long time since Gareth Fenning had looked anything like his picture.

"You don't have the standing to challenge the order."

Emily laughed and waved to Harvey who was sitting on the couch. "It's lovely to speak to you, too, Gareth. I'm doing fine."

"Eh?"

"What's the thing about standing?"

When Gareth spoke again, he sounded on much more comfortable ground. "To contest the court order, you need to have some connection to the woman in question."

"But Agnetha Salem doesn't have any connection to her. How is that fair?"

"According to the documentation filed with the court, she's the woman's guardian. Or was, until she turned eighteen. In the absence of any other relative that trumps a stranger."

Emily walked through to her bedroom and closed the

door. "What kind of relationship would someone need for the court to pay attention?"

"A husband would be best. A sibling, parent, or child would be next on the list."

"She doesn't have those." Emily pulled the puzzle box out of her bag and stared at it, tracing her fingers along its delicate lines. "What about a fiancé?"

Gareth huffed out a breath, then hummed for a few seconds. "It's not a recognised position, usually."

"Just a moment." Emily closed her eyes, thinking back through everything she'd learned in the past few days. Her scar itched and numbness spread up her legs. "What if Sheryl had a falling out with her guardian before the accident? Would that change anything?"

"Who told you that?"

A dead witch. "I don't remember. I've heard so much from so many people lately."

"Unless she emancipated herself through the courts, it doesn't change a thing."

"What about the DNR?"

There was a cautious silence. "What's that?"

"The hospital has a do not resuscitate order on Sheryl Hawthorne. Was that also filed through the courts?"

Another bout of humming. "It could be. More likely, the hospital had a direct conversation with the relative."

"If she is a relative."

"All I can say is I haven't seen anything about emancipation." Gareth sighed and clicked his tongue. "Of course," he admitted, "I didn't actually go looking for that."

"If we found evidence showing Agnetha was no longer Sheryl's guardian, would that invalidate her application?"

Again the low hums and haws. "Perhaps."

"And we could then lodge an application from her fiancé?"

"I think if there were no other relatives, it would fall on the hospital to make submissions in the patient's best interest. They're the experts, after all."

Emily bit her thumbnail as she followed along the likely outcome. If the hospital acted on behalf of Sheryl, it could go either way. First do no harm might be part of the Hippocratic oath but prolonging someone's life via machine without reasonable expectation of recovery wasn't ideal.

Especially since the patient in question was an organ donor.

She didn't need Wanda's concerned presence to feel the sand slipping through the hourglass. No matter which way she turned, Sheryl was running out of time.

"Can you lodge an appeal or injunction or something against the application?"

"As I said, if you don't have standing—"

"Not to succeed, necessarily. Just to buy us some time."

Gareth's voice was far brighter as he responded. "You know you can always count on a lawyer to string something out, especially for the amount I'm going to charge per hour."

Emily laughed despite herself. "What about the friends and family discount? Don't I qualify?"

"We'll see. I'll talk with a few colleagues and work out a path forward. Once we've sorted something out, I'll send you the bill."

"I look forward to it. How long do you think you can stall the decision?"

"A couple of weekdays, easy. Maybe even a few weeks if we're lucky and the judge reserves a decision."

"The longer, the better." Emily managed a weak smile for Wanda as she ended the call.

"That woman shouldn't be allowed to make decisions for my sister. You need to watch your back around her."

Emily realised she had no idea what the time was and

turned the speech function of her watch back on. Almost noon.

"How about we tackle Terrence first? He should be due to take his lunch break from the butcher soon. If we hang about outside, I'm sure we'll catch him."

Peanut jumped into Emily's lap, apparently disapproving of the plan. When Emily stood, he meowed in protest.

"I'll be back soon enough, kitty. Go into the kitchen and try to trip my brother up again why don't you?"

The cat mewed again. Emily could have sworn he had an expression of indignation on his face.

WHEN EMILY POPPED her head into the butcher's shop, she thought her timing was off. The owner of the establishment, Jacky Ribbing, stood by himself behind the counter. A crowd in front of him suggested he'd been that way for a while.

Settling in for a long wait, Emily decided she could pick up a few lamb chops for dinner while she was there. After one quick check in her handbag to ensure she had enough cash, she joined the back of the meandering line.

Luckily, not many new people joined her and when Emily got to the front of the queue, she had the shop pretty much to herself. She placed her order, then said, "Isn't Terrence about? I usually buy my stuff through him."

Jacky shot her a curious glance and Emily flushed. She usually bought all her meat at the supermarket, saving herself an extra trip. At least he was good enough not to mention it.

"The lad didn't turn up for work today. He must be sick because I left a message on his cell and still haven't heard back."

Emily frowned, trying to think. "He did get pretty banged up at the roller derby on Saturday."

"Not really." Jacky wrapped the chops in wax paper and handed them across the counter. "I was there, and I've seen him survive far worse and still turn up for work."

"Has he ever been away sick before?"

"Of course." Jacky frowned. "But that's the thing. He's *called* in sick. I've never known him to just not turn up." He nodded to the man standing behind Emily and started to prepare his order. "It's a bit of a worry, now that I think about it."

She packed the chops in her bag and handed over the exact change. "I'm headed out his way, so I'll drop in and see if he's home."

"If he is, give him a rark up from me, will you? Unless he's in the hospital or something, I expect better."

Apart from a few schoolkids who were probably wagging, there wasn't anybody about on the way out to Terrence's house. As Emily pulled up in front of the property, she frowned. The curtains were still pulled. If he was sitting inside nursing a hangover, he was about to get a shock.

"Terrence!" Emily yelled out as she slammed her hand on the door. After a minute, she moved around to the windows, hoping there'd be a crack in the curtains she could see through. No such luck.

She walked around the side of the house, stopping at a closed gate. With a few quick fumbles, Emily reached through and flicked the catch up from the wrong side. Luckily, it wasn't locked.

The back yard was empty but at least the kitchen and dining-room windows were uncovered. Not that they revealed much of use. Emily stood, with her hands cupped to cut the overhead glare. A chair had fallen onto its side and been left there. When she strained to see further, she saw a bowl overturned on the floor.

With her heart pounding quicker, Emily knocked on the

back door, no longer expecting anyone to answer. She lifted the doormat hoping to see the glint of a spare key, but there was nothing but a few woodlice, scurrying to escape the sudden burst of light.

A row of flower pots also bore no fruit, so she stood on tiptoes and felt along the top of the door jamb. Just as her fingers brushed against metal, someone pounded on the front door.

"Terrence," a woman's voice called. "You come out here, right now. I need to talk to you!"

Emily stepped down and hid her hands behind her back, her cheeks flushing with colour. The insistent knock sounded again, and she looked around her, hoping for a path to escape.

On her right side was a six-foot high fence. On her left, the gate she'd come through. The one which would lead her straight into the path of whoever was pounding on the door.

She shifted a few steps in that direction, ensuring the slats of the fence hid her body from whoever was on the other side. With her head cocked, Emily listened.

"I know you're not at work," the woman continued. "Come to the door right now, or you're in trouble."

There was another thump from the front door, this time sounding more like a kick than a hit.

Emily caught movement and shuffled to the safety of the back-door stoop before the woman could reach the gate. Another kick, then the sound of heavy breathing.

Just as Emily was eyeing the side fence and wondering if she could vault over the top, footsteps led away from the house, soon followed by the slam of a car door.

Back at the gate she peered through a gap in the slats. Although Emily's vision wasn't great, it was good enough to grant her a flash of colour from the driver's seat.

Ginger curls.

The driver was Belinda Bierswack.

Although she'd found the key, the close call left Emily without any desire to venture into the house. She let herself out the gate and locked it behind her, running a hand through her hair while walking to her car.

She'd parked right out in front of the house. What had she been thinking? Belinda must have seen it and even if she didn't know who it belonged to right now, she could easily find out.

"Why would anybody want to know who drives your little Swift?" Emily whispered. "About time you checked your ego."

"Because you were just trying to bust into a stranger's house?" Cynthia said, startling Emily so much her heart skipped a beat and made her glad she hadn't yet turned on the engine.

"I was just looking in the windows. I'm a concerned citizen."

Although Wanda joined her fellow ghost in laughter, Emily realised the words were true. From what she'd learned about Terrence, so recently turning his life around, it was a terrible sign to skip work. Especially when he didn't seem to be at home, either.

"You don't think something bad's happened to him, do you?" she asked.

Wanda pulled at her bloodstained top. "If he's the one behind the burglaries, he deserves it. You should break in and search for the spell book."

"You can go inside and check without breaking any laws," Emily pointed out. "I'm not sure they would have moved it somewhere more visible with another few hours up their sleeve."

"Heads up," Cynthia said, pointing to the nearest intersection. "Or rather, heads down, Witchy-poo. It's your favourite leader."

Emily wished she could duck her head out of sight as Agnetha pulled into the space in front of them. Instead, she got back out of the car and nodded to the woman.

"What're you doing here?"

"I dropped by Terrence's work to apologise for my behaviour yesterday. When the owner told me he wasn't there, I came here instead, but he's not answering the door."

"What?"

Emily frowned and took a step back, wondering which part of her statement the woman hadn't caught. "I went to the butcher—"

"Terrence isn't at work?"

"He didn't turn up and hasn't phoned. Jacky tried to call him, but it went straight to voicemail."

Agnetha's face turned from a reddened snarl into a pale mask of fear. "He was getting ready when I left."

She stared at the house for a long minute, then strode up the front path. When Agnetha unlocked the door, she fumbled with the handle.

Emily thought of Terrence's gang involvement. His stumbles with drugs. If the rumours were true, then the sight awaiting his sister indoors wouldn't be a pleasant one.

She hurried up the path and put a hand on Agnetha's shoulder. "Do you want me to look first?"

The woman nodded, frozen in place as Emily passed by and let her eyes adjust to the dim light. The hallway was clear, as was the dining room and the kitchen. She crossed off room after room, feeling a sense of relief and increasing dread with each one. She hadn't found him yet, but that just made it more likely the next door would hide him.

When the last room proved empty, she walked back

outside the house. "He's not in there. A chair and a bowl are overturned but I can't see any other signs of a struggle."

Agnetha pressed a hand to her abdomen, breathing in and out before she abruptly walked inside. After a few minutes, she returned to the doorway. "There's a smear of blood on the wall of the kitchen. I'm calling the police."

CHAPTER SIXTEEN

Sergeant Winchester's expression fell when he saw Emily standing in the doorway. "Can't you leave these poor folks alone for just a few days?"

"I didn't have anything to do with what's gone on here." She crossed her arms and straightened her spine. "When I went by the butcher shop to apologise to Terrence for last night, he wasn't there. I was just trying him at home when his sister pulled up."

"What time did you leave for work this morning?" the sergeant asked, turning his attention towards Agnetha.

"Ten to eight, same as always."

"Do you always get let out so early?"

She frowned and checked her watch. "I took a half day off to sort some stuff out in Christchurch. When I came home, I found her"—Agnetha jerked her chin at Emily—"parked right outside and no sign of Terrence."

"Can you account for your whereabouts this morning?" Sergeant Winchester directed his gaze back to Emily who sighed.

"At the charity shop, then the tavern, then a clothes shop, then the butcher's, then here."

"Busy morning," he said in a deadpan voice. "Why aren't you at work today?"

"Gregory and Pete weren't happy about me trying to implicate their teammate in a burglary." Emily felt her cheeks growing hot, and was happy when Cynthia rolled her eyes, a welcome distraction. "They said they could handle the weekend donations alone."

"Show me inside, then."

The sergeant and Agnetha disappeared inside and Emily shifted from foot to foot on the stoop. The day was growing colder, an easterly wind blowing straight in from the sea, and she pulled the sleeves of her cardigan down over her hands.

"Come inside," Agnetha called out a few minutes later. "I want you in here where I can keep an eye on you."

"That's why I'm standing out here," Emily muttered under her breath, but followed the woman's directions and moved indoors to stand awkwardly in the dining room.

"There're a few signs of a struggle but nothing much. Had your brother been in contact with his old friends again?" The sergeant raised his eyebrows as he put the question to Agnetha.

"If I thought that for a second, I'd never have left him alone," she snapped back. "As far as I'm aware, he was done with all that."

"Did he make it down to the station to leave his fingerprints?" Emily glanced at the sergeant, then stared at the floor as her peripheral vision caught an angry glare from Agnetha.

"He didn't. Why? Do you think he staged his own kidnapping as a means to avoid giving us evidence?"

"Perhaps." Emily cupped her elbows, shivering. "It's just an idea."

"A foolish idea. I already told you last night, neither of us had anything to do with the burglary."

Emily took a deep breath, then looked up into Agnetha's face. "Belinda didn't seem to think that was the case."

The woman frowned and shrugged. "Who on earth is Belinda?"

Either she was a consummate actress, or the woman really didn't have a clue who Emily was talking about.

"Belinda Bierswack."

Agnetha pulled her mouth down, shaking her head.

"What's she got to do with this?" Sergeant Winchester asked, tapping his notebook with his pen.

"She told me that she'd broken into Jake's house to steal a book on Agnetha's orders."

"Not this again." The woman rolled her eyes. "Neither I nor Terrence had anything to do with any break-ins. We've both got jobs and we're doing nicely." She turned a sharp gaze on the sergeant. "Have you checked with Terrence's bank? If he's been abducted, they might've cleared out his account and run up his credit cards before anybody put a stop on them."

"Give me a minute, I just got here," the sergeant muttered, but he pulled out his phone and moved to the corner of the room for privacy. After he disconnected the call, he gestured for the two ladies to move into the lounge. "It's better if we stay in here until the forensic guys get here. It looks like all the action was confined to the dining room."

"Could I go?" Emily wrinkled her nose at the sergeant. "You already know how to get hold of me if you need to."

"I thought you had the day off work?" Agnetha said before the officer could answer. "If you don't have work, then I'd prefer you to stay right here."

"My brother's in town for a few days. I was planning on spending the day with him."

Sergeant Winchester gave her a narrowed stare. "Right after you spent the morning chasing around after Terrence."

"He was burgled too, you know."

"I do know." Winchester put his hands on his hips. "He was the only one home to answer our call when me and the fingerprints officer came around this morning. Just like we told you we would."

Emily blushed and looked away. In the heat of chasing up the revelations from this morning, she'd completely forgotten. "I should go home and make up that list of stolen items."

"If it was important, you'd have done that already." Agnetha pulled at the sleeve of her cardigan. "You might as well stay."

With a frown, Emily turned to look out the windows, but the curtains were still closed. "Can I open these up? It's gloomy enough in here without shutting out the light."

Sergeant Winchester pulled at the edge of the drapes with his gloved hand until sunlight filled the room. "Better?"

His phone rang before Emily could answer and he turned his back on the two women. Agnetha leaned in closer. "I've heard on the grapevine that you have the same skill as your father."

At the words, Emily jerked back. While the woman stared intently into her face, she looked back through into the dining room where Cynthia stood. Wanda was no doubt still hiding from the Supreme in the car.

"Well?"

"What do you know about my father?"

"I know he could talk to the spirits of the dead. If you can do that, it should be a matter of minutes to find Terrence. Someone on the other side must know where he went. They've got more eyes than us."

Emily traced the length of the scar running down her face. "That's not how it works."

"How does it work, then? Find my brother and I'll reward you handsomely."

"I'm good, thanks."

Agnetha narrowed her eyes. "Really? You don't want a helping hand with all those bone fragments dancing around inside your skull?"

"How did you—?"

The Supreme laughed and Emily suddenly saw it. Saw her power. Minutes before, she'd just been a worried sister but now the energy was pouring from every cell in her body. Agnetha was more alive than anybody Emily had ever seen.

"I know everything about everyone in this community." She leaned closer, her warm breath caressing the side of Emily's cheek. "Your doctors gave up on you, but I wouldn't. I can cure you. All I want in return is my brother."

Emily's hands jerked up, an automatic gesture of protection. "I don't know what happened to Terrence."

"Ask your dead friends."

"There are only two of them at the moment and neither of them knows what happened either. They're a couple of ghosts who haven't moved on to the next realm, not some all-seeing all-knowing creatures."

Agnetha sighed. "What a disappointment. Still, the offer stands, even if you have to use earthly powers to locate him. I know you've played some hand in Terrence's disappearance." She tipped her head towards the sergeant, still engrossed in his phone conversation. "So does he."

"I haven't!" Emily pulled at the neck of her blouse. Where she'd been cold before now the room was stifling hot.

"Why were you here, then?"

Agnetha's eyes drilled into her and Emily took a step back.

"You're kidding," the Supreme said, her lip curling in disgust. "You still think my brother robbed your pathetic little home. Why? What do you have that you think either of us wants?"

"A book of spells."

"I don't need a book to create a spell." Agnetha sneered as she tilted her head to one side, eyes narrowing. "What do you take me for?"

"There's a man in town who'll say different. He'll say you asked him about it specifically, not long before it was stolen."

The Supreme stepped back, her mouth dropping open in surprise. She recovered quickly. "If this is all just following-up on what Jake the Snake is meant to have laid his hands on, I'll save you the bother. He never had the book in the first place."

"There's a lot of people going to a lot of trouble if the spell book doesn't exist."

"Even if you did find it, I'll warn you right now not to mess about with what's written inside. From someone who's had more than her fair share of cleaning up after other people, you want to stay clear of magic dealing with life and death."

"It's not." Emily flicked a glance at Cynthia and squared her shoulders. "We're just putting something back where it belongs."

"If you really want to enact power over mortality," Agnetha continued as though Emily hadn't spoken, "then you should quit fighting against my power of medical attorney. I presume it's on your direction a lawyer suddenly took an interest today."

"What of it?"

"An organ donor bringing new life and hope to seriously ill people is its own magic. Maybe you should think long and hard about that before you're led astray by tales of restoring life to someone who's certified brain dead."

"What would you know?"

Agnetha gave a sad smile. "I'd know that I loved and cared for Wanda and Sheryl Hawthorne years before you even knew their names. I don't care what you think of me, I looked out for those two when nobody else would."

Emily had no rebuttal for those bare truths. Whatever fall-out Wanda thought had happened between Agnetha and her sister, the details were wisps of smoke compared to the hard facts.

As she struggled to find something to say, Sergeant Winchester hung up his call. "That was the officer who looked through your brother's bank accounts."

"Well?" Agnetha turned to face him. "What did they have to say? Has his credit card been used today?"

The sergeant nodded at Emily. "Are you sure you want to share this conversation?"

After a second, the woman returned her gaze to Emily. "Fine. You can go. As you said, the sergeant knows how to get in touch if you're needed."

She didn't stick around to be told twice. As she slammed her car door, Wanda popped up from the back seat.

"How'd it go?"

"It's a mess," Emily admitted. "Terrence is missing and Agnetha somehow knows all about me. She wants me to track him down and return him."

"Like you've got him stashed away somewhere?" Wanda gave a dismissive toss of her head. "She must be desperate."

"Oh, thanks!"

"I didn't mean—"

"Move over Witchy-poo." Cynthia appeared in the back seat, looking like the cat who'd got into the cream. "I have a bit of news."

"I'm not sure I want to hear anything more," Emily said. "All I want is to get home and pretend the last few days never happened."

"You'll want to hear this," Cynthia insisted. "The sergeant just told Agnetha her brother's bank account hasn't been touched."

"Fascinating," Emily murmured, directing her attention to the intersection they were approaching.

"That bit's not, but this is. Apparently, he's got a bank balance of over one hundred grand." Cynthia sat back, an expression of satisfaction on her face. "A bit hard to save that up from a job at the butcher's, don't you think?"

CHAPTER SEVENTEEN

Emily stared at Jake's yard, the twisting heaps of metal glinting with evil in the afternoon light. Agnetha's scornful words played out in her mind again. *He never had the book in the first place.*

Could that be true?

Her mind fast-forwarded through the action on the day she'd come to visit. His surprise had been genuine, surely? When Jake went up that attic staircase to find the book missing, it had caught him off-guard.

She exited the car, wincing at the noise of the door closing in the still afternoon. When he'd called to say their appointment today was off—furious she'd called the police and mentioned his name—Emily had been too surprised to protest.

Now, the vehement cancellation appeared strange. Of course, he had every right to be upset with her bandying his name about, but if Jake had been as frantic to retrieve the spell book and save his girlfriend's life as she and Wanda were, he'd be over it.

"He's not there," a man called out from over the road. "There's no use knocking."

Emily shuffled across the road, checking for traffic even though they were at a dead end. "Has he gone to work?"

"He took off late last night," the neighbour said. He'd been turning the earth in his front garden and now slipped his gloved hand along the blade of a small fork, throwing the dirt back into the flowerbed. "It made an awful racket. Motorbikes and souped-up cars." He shook his head. "I'm glad I'm past all that."

"Did you recognise anybody?"

"Just some gang. I wasn't familiar with the patches on their jackets."

"A gang?" Emily thought of Terrence's troubled past. "Did Jake go with them willingly?"

The man huffed out a breath of air, looking amused. "I didn't pay that much attention. I only looked out the window 'cause they woke me up. When I went across the road to complain, he didn't answer."

Emily thanked the man and got back into her car, wondering what she could do next.

"You should wait until that old fellow heads back inside, then break-in," Wanda said firmly. "If he's still got my book, then you're entitled to retrieve it."

"No, I'm not." Emily sighed and pulled the car out, heading home. "Just because he lied to me doesn't give me property rights. Either he bought it from the auction fair and square, or someone's been lying to us and he never had it."

"What next, then?" Cynthia arched her right eyebrow. "Are you planning on roping in legions of the undead to do your bidding and track down Terrence?"

While Wanda stared on in confusion, Emily dismissed her interest with a flap of her hand. Part of her wished she could do exactly that while the other half never wanted to see another ghost again.

"I DON'T SUPPOSE you're familiar with any gangs?" Emily asked her brother over dinner. "Unless I can find out what happened to Terrence or Jake, I seem to be at a dead end."

"You can't just give up," Wanda said in horror. "Remember my sister's life is on the line."

"Not my crowd," Harvey said, shaking his head. "You've met the dodgiest person I know in Pinetar already. Aside from that, everyone I know stays on the right side of the law."

"Why don't you ask Crystal?"

Emily snapped a loaded glance at Cynthia for the idea, but it appeared the ghost was genuine.

"She knows everybody in Pinetar and half of Ashburton. If anyone is going to be friends with someone in a biker gang, it'll be her."

The idea held some appeal, but it would have to wait until morning. Even resting up for a few hours on the couch hadn't restored her energy.

Imagine if Agnetha took care of that for you. Hey, presto! All your bone fragments and your troubles would be gone.

Emily shook her head, but the idea stayed. As she lay in bed, not sleeping, the thought of all she'd be able to do if the injuries from her car accident were taken away recurred. She could go back to Christchurch, return to the job she loved. Harvey could keep this house, she wouldn't care.

You'd lose Peanut. And Cynthia.

As much as she wanted to say good riddance to at least one of those, Emily had to admit she'd miss the two equally. Despite the odds, she and Cynthia had become good friends.

But you wouldn't need to rely on friends if you got back to normal. You could rely on yourself.

She could live alone again, with no one except her clients or coworkers to care what happened to her. Emily's mind played out the scenario, unsure if that would be a nightmare or pure bliss.

You could read a book. By yourself. Without having to endure someone else's idea of the perfect narrator.

Reading had always been a comfort and her favourite pastime. Even with audiobooks and comic strips on offer, it wasn't the same.

As Emily drifted closer to sleep, she thought of her old life. Quiet. Intellectually challenging. Everything shaped to fit exactly what she needed.

You don't even know how to find Terrence, you dimwit. The offer isn't going to matter.

With that thought occupying her mind, Emily finally managed to fall asleep.

"No, I don't know any gangs." Crystal sounded put out and when Emily's watch announced the time, she realised why.

"Sorry to barge in so early," she said, blushing at the thought she'd turned up on her friend's doorstep before six o'clock. "I just couldn't sleep for thinking about what might have happened."

Crystal yawned with her mouth so wide, she appeared to have a flip-top head. "If you're worried, go to the police."

"They're already involved," Emily said, wringing her hands. "But I thought if we could follow up some of our own leads, we might solve the situation more quickly."

"You know, I'm usually one for butting my nose into a situation where it's not wanted," Crystal said, walking into the kitchen and flicking the switch on the coffee-maker. "But even I think this might be one time we should stand back and let them do their job."

"I suppose. It just makes me feel so useless when I can't get stuck in and help."

"Better to stand on the sidelines than bolt onto the field and upset the entire game."

Emily stared at her friend with suspicion. "Who is this level-headed person and what have you done with Crystal?"

"If you want to get the benefit of full Crystaliciousness, you need to let me get a good sleep-in."

By the time Emily had drunk her fill of coffee, her watch announced it was seven-thirty and her stomach sloshed as she walked out the door.

"Now, what?"

"Break into Jake's house and check it for spells," Wanda suggested again.

"I'm not doing that. Next idea, please."

"Go home and get some rest." Cynthia stretched her arms over her head. "You're making me feel tired and I don't even need to sleep."

Instead, Emily headed for the charity shop. It was too early for either Gregory or Pete to be there, but it suited her just fine. She tutted her way through all the boxes they'd half-unpacked the day before, then set the treasures she'd unearthed in a row.

Seeing the line-up of antiques reminded her that she hadn't yet completed a list of stolen items. Nothing of value had gone, but whoever rummaged through the wooden chest she kept on her bedside cabinet had removed half a dozen pieces of costume jewellery worth precisely nothing.

She didn't really want it back but if it helped the police to lay charges, it was worth the effort.

As she let herself in through the front door, Emily heard

Harvey cooking in the kitchen. She smiled as he sang through half a dozen lines of Pokarekare Ana with not a single original lyric intact.

"Pancakes?" he called out.

"I'll pass." Emily sat at the table, happy to watch him cooking. "I've had so many cups of coffee already, there's no room for food."

"You'll end up with high blood pressure at this rate," Harvey warned, dolloping some cream and jam on one side of his plate with abandon.

"Better than high cholesterol."

"Is it, though? This is certainly more fun."

She opened her mouth to ask about missing items when her phone rang. Gareth's voice yelled out of the speaker, so Emily had to hold the phone away from her ear.

"The judge wants to consider the motion this morning. Get your skates on. You and your boy need to be here by ten sharp."

"I thought you said it would buy us a few days."

"I was wrong. It doesn't happen often, but it does happen. Can you get here in time?"

"Jake's missing."

"Who's Jake?" There was a short pause, then, "Oh, right. Never mind. The whole thing's a long shot, anyway. Are you able to make it?"

"If I can't, would that postpone it for another day?"

Gareth laughed as though she'd just told an uproarious joke during the middle of happy hour. "Not a chance. He'll just dismiss it out of hand. If you want to stretch the decision out by a few hours, you'll be here. Ten o'clock. Court two."

He'd hung up by the time Emily got her head on straight. She leapt to her feet and hurried through to the bedroom. What was appropriate for visiting a friend in the wee hours of the morning wouldn't do for presenting evidence in front of a judge.

She hauled a dark blue woollen suit out of the back of her wardrobe and gave it a sniff. No moths. Good.

With the addition of a high-collared white blouse, she was soon ready.

Emily didn't have the slightest idea of what she could say to convince a judge, but it was Sheryl's life on the line. She'd better think of something in the hour-long drive to Christchurch.

CHAPTER EIGHTEEN

Emily stood in the small courtroom, frustration welling inside her. "But you can't just kill her!"

Gareth winced beside her, while the judge cleared his throat before saying, "Nobody is killing anyone, Miss Curtis. We're here to deliberate on the validity of your motion."

"It's what the end—"

"Mr Fenning, please get control of your client. I will not accept outbursts of this nature in my courtroom."

Emily opened her mouth to retort but Gareth elbowed her in the ribs hard enough to know he meant business.

"I'm sorry, your honour. This is a very emotional subject and I'm afraid my client let her distress get the better of her. She won't call out again."

Gareth dragged Emily back into a sitting position beside him. "Don't embarrass me," he whispered out of the side of his mouth. "I have to come in here for work every day, remember?"

She buttoned her lip but couldn't quite go so far as to say she was sorry. To listen to Judge Fortimer's monotone deliberation drove her up the wall. Considering it was a human life they were discussing, someone should be emotional.

"I can see no standing for this injunction to be granted." The judge flicked through the pages in front of him, then laid them on the bench, hands folded on top of them. "I understand that you might have a friendship with Miss Hawthorne and this matter will be very painful, but the law is clear. Only those with a legally recognised relationship with the patient have the right to decide upon her care."

Emily closed her eyes, knowing what was coming next but still dreading the words.

"The motion for an injunction is denied."

As they left the courtroom, Emily's anger bubbled over. "How does an old man in robes get to say if Sheryl lives or dies? How is that fair?"

"He doesn't." Gareth grabbed Emily's arm before she could walk straight onto the road. "Watch out! This isn't Pinetar, you know. Pedestrians give way to traffic here, not the other way around."

"What do you call that, then?" She waved her hand back towards the court building.

"I call that a judge deciding who is in a position to make the best decisions regarding medical care for a woman who can no longer make those choices for herself." Gareth glared at her for a moment, then sighed. "He isn't telling the hospital what to do. He's just pointing out that her legal next-of-kin has more rights than you do. Big surprise."

"If they wanted to make things fair, they should recognise me as the next-of-kin," Wanda called out. "Just because I'm dead doesn't mean I don't have Sheryl's best interests at heart."

But Gareth would think she was even more mental than he did already if Emily passed that particular message on. Instead, she pursed her lips to express her displeasure.

"Did you want to go to lunch and catch up?"

Emily gave Gareth a careful look and shook her head. He appeared so relieved at that answer, she laughed. "I'll let you get back to work. Thanks for all your help. I know I seem ungrateful at the moment, but I do appreciate your time."

"Your cheque attached to the invoice I'm going to send you is all the appreciation I need." Gareth waved goodbye and hurried across the intersection, disappearing into a tall building swarming with suited men and women.

There was a bench outside the lobby and Emily sat to gather her thoughts. Although she'd known from the beginning her application to the court would be denied, it was galling how quickly the judge had dismissed it. With all the world caught up with red tape, it didn't seem fair Sheryl's had been cut through as quickly as that.

She put her head in her hands, resting until a man asked if she was all right. After that, Emily felt conspicuous sitting there, so stood up and hobbled away, her hip complaining loudly she'd been too active for the past few days.

Her old accounting firm was nearby, and Emily walked there, her feet guiding her subconsciously through the journey she'd made so many times before. Standing outside, she felt the loss of her old life too keenly to stay for long.

Without paying much attention, she soon found herself outside a block of flats, not far away from her old job. With a start, Emily remembered these were where Terrence told her he used to live before moving to Pinetar, Ermine Villas. She searched the nameplates but couldn't find his old listing.

"Are you looking for someone, dear?"

Emily spun on her heel to find an elderly woman with long black hair and an eager expression staring back. "A—A friend of mine used to live here," she stammered. "I wasn't sure if he'd moved on or not."

"What's the name?" The woman pushed past Emily and

held the main gate open, waving her through. "I've been here for the last twenty years, so I can remember everyone who's spent time here."

"Terrence Salem," Emily answered, then scrunched her face up as she wondered at the politeness of including the most relevant physical description.

"The Down's Syndrome kid?" the woman replied, saving Emily the debate.

"Yes, that's him."

"He moved on a while ago." The woman unlocked a door with a series of three keys, then paused to look back at Emily. "You're welcome to come in and share a cup of tea if you've got time to waste."

"That sounds great."

While the woman busied herself in the kitchen, Emily took a seat in the well-appointed lounge. "You have a lovely home."

"Thanks. It's staying in one place for too long that does it. I've never had to thin out my collection or decide what to keep or throw away, prior to packing my life into little boxes. Milk?"

"Yes, please." Emily leaned to her right to examine a tea chest inlaid with mother-of-pearl, edged with gold filigree. "I work in a donation shop in Pinetar. We get through a lot of the 'throw away' boxes you mentioned."

"Oh, everyone's into downsizing these days, aren't they? Mark my words, give the world time and they'll swing back to being hoarders. It always goes from one extreme to another."

"I'm sure you're right."

"Sorry, I'm being rude," the woman said, positioning a cup of tea on the side table nearest Emily. "I haven't even introduced myself. Gladys Ranger."

"And I'm Emily Curtis. It's nice to meet you."

"Now, this boy you wanted to talk about, I think he moved on about a year ago. Maybe two."

"That sounds like him," Emily agreed. "Did you know Terrence very well?"

"Goodness no." Gladys cackled with laughter, thumping her chest as she broke into a fit of coughing. "This is the city, dear. Nobody knows each other very well here. That's one of the reasons I'm so fond of it."

Emily couldn't help but return her smile. Small town life meant living in each other's pockets. Although the attention was helpful for someone with a condition like hers, it did grow wearying. Especially considering her introverted nature.

"What else did you know about Terrence?"

"Hm." Gladys took a sip of her tea and Emily followed suit.

The taste was mellow, eased further with the addition of milk. She tasted a hint of orange blossoms, so much fancier than what she was used to at home.

"He was a very friendly fellow. Once, he helped me out with my groceries when I was struggling to hold them all and unlock the door."

"That's nice. You don't often get chivalrous acts these days."

"You certainly don't." Gladys frowned. "He had a girlfriend for a while. Beautiful woman. I'm not sure what happened there, but she hung around here almost every day then poof, she was gone."

Emily frowned. "Are you talking about a slightly older woman?"

"Goodness, no. He had a sister if that's who you're implying, and she was a crotchety thing. Terrence lived two doors along but if his sister was staying over, I could hear them arguing clear as a bell. She wanted him to move in with her after their parents left town. He wanted to stay put, and I can't blame him."

"What was the girlfriend like?"

The smile returned to Gladys's face. "A real sweetie. She was always in a sundress or a skirt and twinset. A real girly-girl, if you know what I mean. Given the way the two of them carried on, I thought for sure there'd be wedding bells." She gave a long sigh, then sipped at her tea again. "Shows what I know."

After finishing her cup, Emily replaced it in the saucer. Her hands were shaking enough that it chittered on the edge before settling into the groove. "I heard he became involved with a bad crowd."

"The bikers?"

Emily nodded.

Gladys sat back and tapped a fingernail on the side of her teacup. "I guess they were a bit rough. Still, they were as polite as pie to me. Once, they jumped over the fence and I caught them. Told the leader I'd phone the police. He apologised and made his mates all vault back onto the footpath."

"I'm not sure breaking into a place, then breaking back out qualifies as polite."

"Compared to bashing my head in as a lesson on how to speak to them?"

Emily's eyes widened at the violent image her words conjured up.

Gladys gave a bark of laughter. "I've heard of that and worse. It's a dangerous business, being old and opinionated. Those guys might dress in leathers but that's where their hard exterior stops." She pulled at her bottom lip for a moment. "Although, I'm also sure it was them that killed my azaleas, going to the bathroom outside, so they weren't that great."

"Do you know the name of the gang?" When Gladys's

brow wrinkled at the request, Emily explained, "I'm trying to track down Terrence. He disappeared from his house early yesterday, and nobody's seen him since."

"Young men like to take themselves off from time to time. I wouldn't worry."

"The police are worried." Emily paused, tapping a finger against her bottom lip. "There was some blood in his house and other signs of a struggle. We think he might've been abducted against his will."

"And you think the gang had something to do with that?" Gladys shook her head. "No. I would swear on a stack of bibles that wasn't the case."

"He used to run drugs for them," Emily said. "Whether they're good or bad at heart, dealing in that field runs a lot of risks. It'd be nice if I could make sure they don't know anything about it before I head back to Pinetar."

"It doesn't matter." Gladys sat forward, hands linked over her crossed knee. "Even if I wanted to tell you the name of the gang, I don't know it. I don't have a clue where you'd find them, or even where to begin looking."

With a frustrated sigh, Emily stood up and paced over to the window. A woman walked by, on the other side of the wrought iron fencing, a large Crusader sign on the back of her denim jacket.

"What about insignia?" She turned back and stared at Gladys with raised eyebrows. "Do you remember any emblems or slogans the gang wore on their jackets?"

"I—" Gladys broke off and walked into the kitchen, returning a moment later with a pen and pad. "They had a patch sewn on their shoulders, like this." She held out the drawing, her face worried.

"Thank you." Emily took a picture and told her phone to perform an image search. "I must go but I'm grateful you took the time to talk to me."

Gladys laughed as she escorted her to the door. “Oh, please. I’m an old woman living alone in the city so I’m pretty sure the thanks should go the opposite way.”

Her phone binged a few moments later. Mortal Guises. Headquarters on Linwood Avenue.

CHAPTER NINETEEN

"You must be mental, thinking you can walk in there and expecting they'll let you walk out again in one piece." Cynthia lifted her nose and sniffed her disdain.

"If you heard Gladys, then you'll know they're not likely to hurt an old woman."

"One incident that happened in a nice part of town when they were trespassing on the property and probably laden with drugs." Wanda sat forward, crossing her arms on the back of the seat. "It's nice you want to take such risks to help my sister, but it'll be even more helpful if you don't end up dead."

"Unless you have a better idea, then I suggest you stop shooting down my plan." Emily flipped the rear-view mirror down to examine her face, pulling her hair back so her scar was on full display. "Right now, we have one lead on Terrence and he's the only reasonable suspect in the theft of the book. I'm not seeing many other options."

"Just for the record, I don't care if you kill yourself. I'm just opposed to floating all the way back to Pinetar by myself."

"So sweet." Emily blew Cynthia a kiss. "And you won't be by yourself. I'm sure Wanda will be with you every step of the way."

An exaggerated eye roll later, and Emily stood at the corrugated iron fence that served as the Mortal Guises front door. She couldn't work out which part to thump upon, so gave it a kick instead.

Rust particles showered onto her feet. It had been eight years since her last tetanus booster, and she hoped it meant she was still protected. Ending the day in the emergency department for any reason would be bad enough. For something that was her own fault? Worst case scenario.

"Come on. There's no one there." Wanda floated beside Emily, wringing her hands.

"Would you do me a favour?"

"Of course." Wanda's face transposed into a beaming smile. "What do you need?"

"Could you float over the other side and see if anyone's home? It would be nice to know I'm not risking lockjaw for nothing."

"Already done, Scarface. There's three in the front room, but you'll have to knock a lot louder than that. They've all got headphones on, working on their PlayStation tan."

Emily took a step back, then aimed a high-kick at the metal door. She gave a screech as pain sank its fangs deep into her hip.

"You'll be hurting tomorrow, either way, Scarface. Man up."

Another kick and Cynthia gave her a thumbs up. "They're coming."

She had to take a hanky out of her bag to wipe the tears away before a gigantic hulk of a man answered the door.

"What's up?"

"Can I come in?" Emily asked in her sweetest old-granny voice. "I want to speak to your leader."

"Why?" The man stuck his head out, scanning the footpath in either direction. "Who sent you? Is this a wind-up?"

"Nobody sent me. I just need to have a word with whoever's in charge. I'm presuming that's not you."

The giant folded his arms and shot her a grumpy look. "I might be the leader here, for all you know. Tell me your business, or you're not getting through this door."

Cynthia mugged Emily from behind the giant's back, then picked up a game controller from a table near the door and threw it at the back of the man's head.

"What the…? Was that you, Gary?"

"Nah, mate." The man in question didn't even look up, just continued to stare at the screen. "Hurry up."

"Yeah," Emily echoed. "Hurry up. Let me in."

"Whatever." The man rubbed the back of his neck and Emily saw a red weal forming there as he turned away. "Get in. I'll call Slim down for you."

Cynthia winked at Emily as she walked through the makeshift door and she felt reassured by the poltergeist's company. She pulled her phone out of her pocket and set it to record, then balance it on an exposed beam halfway up the wall.

"He's coming," the large man said, returning to his seat in front of the screen. "I hope you don't regret it."

"You'll regret it," Gary snarled, launching his body from side to side as his avatar performed an athletic manoeuvre on the screen.

A man aged in his late forties sloped out of a back room, rubbing at his hair. It stuck up on end, pointing in all directions. Although the voice of manners her mother had instilled in Emily insisted she move to meet him halfway, the thought of her phone's reach kept her standing near the door.

"Pig said you wanted something."

"I do. Slim, is it?"

He nodded, his lanky frame agreeing even if he hadn't. "Do I know you?"

"You know a friend of mine. Terrence Salem?"

Emily kept a close watch on Slim's face, but it gave nothing away. The man's features stayed composed as he said, "Who's that, then?"

"He ran drugs for you."

"Drugs?" Slim stared at her for a full second, then burst into laughter. "Oh, no, lady. You don't get us as easy as that. We don't have anything to do with drugs, here. We don't need no runners because we don't deal, we don't take, and we don't supply."

He turned as though that ended the conversation, but Emily took a step closer, putting a hand on his arm. "You know Terrence, don't you?"

"Yeah." Slim shook her off. "What of it? He moved out of town a while ago. We barely see him anymore."

"You've seen him recently."

That caused a reaction, a slight widening of the eyes and lifting of the man's brow. Emily's stomach gave a jump.

"I don't know what you're talking about, lady, but you're in my home without an invitation, making all sorts of accusations. I don't like it."

"I'm not making—"

"Just said we were running drugs, didn't you?"

Emily sucked in her bottom lip. "Somebody told me that's what you did."

"We don't have nothing to do with that business. There's enough to occupy us with legitimate enterprises. We don't need to mess about with illegal stuff, and we never have."

"What did Terrence do for you, then?"

Slim took a half-step back, his lip curling. "Lady, I don't know who you are, but I'm not standing in my own home answering questions for nobody. You want to ask me something, put it in writing."

"Please," Emily called out as the man turned to go. "I know you were in Pinetar the other night. A man saw you at the residence of Jake the Snake."

"Jake the Snake." Slim scoffed at the moniker. "I don't know anybody of that—"

"Your bikes were seen down the end of Alberton Lane. If you make me come back here with the police to ask the same questions, I will. I'm just trying to be expedient."

"You what?" Slim stared at her with a puzzled expression.

"She means quick," Gary called out from the floor.

"Don't threaten me," Slim said, taking a menacing step forward. "From what you've just said, you're here alone and you haven't told the police anything about us. If you like, I could ask Pig here to take care of you and I could go back into my room to sleep in peace."

"I'm live streaming."

"Eh?" Slim's eyes flicked over to Gary, who shrugged this time. "You're what?"

"This entire encounter is being recorded live and streamed on Facebook. If you hurt me, the police'll take about five minutes to piece it all together, then they'll be knocking down your door."

"It's not legal to record a video without consent," Gary called out.

"And it's not legal to threaten someone's life. Didn't stop you."

Slim held up a finger. "Wait, a minute. I didn't say that. I said they'd take care of you. It could mean anything."

"Like a day at the spa?" Emily stared at him, her face an expressionless mask.

"Exactly."

"We've got two men missing in Pinetar and you're the only lead I've got. How about you stop spouting rubbish and start telling me what you know?"

"Who's missing?"

"Terrence Salem and Jake the Snake."

"Downtime is missing?" Slim stared at her, raising his finger as he half-closed his eyes.

"Nice nickname." Cynthia moved to the wall and stared at Emily's mobile phone. "You forgot to press record, Scarface."

Emily bit her lip, thankful she was the only one who could hear Cynthia's helpful pointer.

"Look, we drove out to Pinetar, the night before last, sure. Terrence phoned us and asked if we could give this man a little scare. We revved the engines and beeped and stuff, enough to wake the neighbours up so they could give him grief. We would've torn up his lawn with our bikes, too, except the whole thing looked like a death trap."

"What then?"

"Then nothing. That's all we did. We didn't even see Terrence that night, just talked to him on the phone."

"Who's taken him?" Pig asked, grunting loudly as he stood up from the floor and walked over to join them. "Our boy didn't say he was in any trouble, did he?"

Slim shook his head. "Just that someone was messing around with his plans and it would help if he had some encouragement to back off. We thought it was done and dusted with the drive by."

"Wait. You're not saying we had anything to do with it, are you?" Pig looked appalled at the thought. "We didn't even see Jake. He was just a shadow behind the curtains."

"It would've taken a lot more than a phone call to arrange a kidnapping," Slim said.

The calm delivery made Emily feel inexplicably better, despite the subject matter.

"Too right," Pig agreed.

Emily looked from one man to the other. "What plans were being messed with?"

Slim shuffled his feet, hands on his hips. "I don't think that's relevant."

Help came from an unexpected source as Pig stepped forward. "Hey, man. Our boy's missing. Maybe it's time to lighten up on the secret squirrel."

"How much do you know about Terrence's family?"

"Not much," Emily admitted. "I only met him for the first time on Saturday."

Slim pulled Pig away, and they talked together in low voices, their tones urgent.

Taking a punt, Emily called out, "Is this to do with his sister being the leader of the local coven? I know that much."

With a narrowed glance, Slim took a step closer to her again. "You believe in that stuff?"

She exchanged an amused glance with Cynthia. "Yeah. I've been forced to believe in a lot of stuff since moving to Pinetar. I might not understand what you're about to tell me, but I can promise you I'll listen with an open mind."

"These witches, they have rules, yeah?"

Emily thought of Agnetha's warning about messing with matters of life and death. "Sure, I can see why they'd need to have guidelines in place."

"One of them is they're not allowed to cast love spells or sell romantic potions." Slim gave her a wink. "On account of all the 'female rights' and stuff the media pays attention to nowadays."

"You mean sexually assaulting people by using a drug to

alter their consciousness? I'm pretty sure that's nothing new. Check out the crimes act."

"Yeah. Well, Downtime thought Jake might be messing around with that stuff."

"Ugh." Emily shivered and wished she could step into the shower. "He forced someone to fall in love with him? That's so gross."

"I don't understand all the ins and outs of it, but we were more than happy to give the man a scare since he didn't really count as a man."

Emily nodded. "But you really don't know what's happened to Terrence, or who might've taken him?"

"Not a clue."

"Perhaps, then, you'd like to explain why he had a hundred thousand dollars sitting in his account. I know that came from you."

CHAPTER TWENTY

"I swear, there's no way we ever gave that amount of money to Downtime." Slim's expression changed from astonished to amused in one blink. "Even if I'd wanted to dump a load on the little man, that kind of wad is out of our reach."

Emily tipped her head back, eyeing the two men down the length of her nose. A gesture that had only made it into her repertoire courtesy of long hours in the company of Cynthia Pettigrew.

"Where else would he get it from, then?"

"The same place he always got his money." Pig gave a snorting laugh, hinting at the reason for his nickname. "Downtime's lucky. It sounds like a joke but that's the truth. There's never been a spin he couldn't ace or a hand he couldn't bluff."

"You're saying he made his money at the casino?"

Slim shrugged. "I can't say for sure. His sister got her knickers in a knot about it a few years ago, said it wasn't any different from casting a love spell."

"She equates love with money?"

"He explained if you take money from the casino, they have to source it from somewhere. That means a lot of people who otherwise would've won, lose."

At the face she pulled, Slim laughed and held up his hands. "I didn't make the rules. Just passing them on."

"So you think he came up to Christchurch to gamble and win on occasion?"

"If he's got unexplained money in his bank account, that's my best guess. Unless you think he was selling his body?"

"Ugh. Enough." Emily held her hands up in a gesture of surrender. "Why would he need all that money? He must've been planning something."

"Planning to get away from his sister, is what I'd guess. She talked up a sob story to get him to go back home but a fool could see it wouldn't last. He wanted to go back there just long enough to sort it out with his girl, then split."

"He doesn't get on with his sister?" Emily was starting to believe Agnetha didn't mesh with anybody. She frowned at the floor, squinting her eyes as she tried to think. "But the money is untouched. He wouldn't build it up just to leave it there when he moved on. Is there anything else you can think of that might point to where he's gone?"

Pig stepped forward. "There's nobody here would ever wish Downtime harm." He socked a fist into his other hand. "If you do find him and want to teach somebody a lesson, you remember we're here."

THE CAR JOURNEY back to Pinetar passed without incident and Emily was soon pulling up outside her home. The door was locked, Harvey gone somewhere without leaving a note. She lay on the sofa, stretching her legs out and massaging her thighs.

"What now?" Wanda shoved her face close. "Perhaps we should pay Agnetha another visit?"

"And ask her what?" Emily sighed. "If it's true her brother disliked her? That sounds like a great way to get kicked out. Until something more happens, we won't get anywhere."

"You can't just lie there!"

Emily rubbed her eyes and sat up. Wanda was right about that. If she did nothing, she'd drive herself around the bend by the end of the day.

"I might check back at the shop and see if they're willing to let me work there again."

"But how will that help?" Wanda floated back and forth in front of Emily, a ghostly version of pacing.

"It will help take my mind off everything and pass the time until there's something new to go on."

She let herself out of the house and walked to the shop, turning a deaf ear to Wanda's pleas. The gang had been her last best hope. She couldn't even think of where to go next.

"Knock, knock," she said, walking into the store and waving to Pete. "Am I forgiven?"

Gregory poked his head out of the back corridor. "Were you in here last night? Everything upstairs looks a lot better organised than I left it."

"I just came in for a few minutes. I hope that's okay."

Pete sighed. "Of course, it's okay. I'm sorry we chased you out of here yesterday. Did you hear the news about Terrence?"

"That he's disappeared? Yes." Emily nodded, not willing to add her own involvement in that discovery to the conversation. "Have you heard any news?"

"No. His sister's absolutely frantic and the police have been around here twice to ask questions." Pete leaned his elbows on the counter. "I think they're at a loss."

"Did they think you were hiding him in a back room or something?"

"Probably. I made a mistake the first time and told them he hadn't ever been in the store, then I remembered he came along with me on Saturday and met you here."

"That's right." Emily hugged herself. "I bumped into him coming down the stairs."

At the prompt, Pete frowned, tapping his fingernail on the bench.

"What is it?" Emily asked after a few minutes. "You've obviously thought of something."

"He had a bag with him when he came in," Pete said. "I thought it was full of his skating gear but when he got into the car, it was empty, and he stuffed it under the seat."

"It wasn't his skating gear," Gregory said, joining them at the counter. "He keeps all of that at the community hall because Agnetha used to get upset when she saw it around the house. She goes mental when she thinks he's in danger of being hurt, so he got a locker."

Emily made her way out the back of the shop, her heart beating harder. "You thought he'd lost his way to the bathroom," she said, exploring the memory and hoping she wasn't embellishing it. "But when I asked him what he was doing upstairs, he didn't say a word." She climbed up the stairs, eagle eyes scanning in all directions.

"He didn't leave anything in the attic room," Gregory said. "It was empty except for the new boxes we dragged up yesterday."

"I'd cleared it out on Friday," Emily agreed. "I got sick of opening things up that I'd already searched through."

At the top of the stairs was an alcove. It held a stack of rugs, which had originally adorned the floor in the attic room, but she'd moved outside because the boxes kept snagging them.

She knelt down, ignoring the warning from her knees that they wouldn't enjoy standing up again. With Gregory's help, they lifted aside the top rugs and exposed a thick book. The cover made from engraved leather. The leaves held shut with a gold chain.

As Emily gasped, Wanda sobbed in relief.

The spell book.

Under her nose all the time.

CHAPTER TWENTY-ONE

As Emily shuffled downstairs, cradling the tome in her arms like a delicate child, Pete followed close behind her.

"We should take that to the police," he said. "They might be able to tie it into Terrence's disappearance."

"Not likely, since he hid it here on Saturday." Emily laid it on the counter, out of the direct sunlight. The engravings marked into the leather were picked out in differing shades of gold, appearing to shift. "It's beautiful."

"It doesn't belong to you." Pete moved to take hold of the volume and Emily slapped his hands away.

"No, but it belongs to Jake, and he was happy to let me use it, considering we both wanted the same thing. Unless you have some evidence revoking his permission, then I think my needs trump yours."

"But he's right," Gregory said in a low voice. "If Terrence stole this book, his disappearance might be connected."

"I've already told the police all about Terrence and Jake." Emily kept her hands firmly pressed against the book, feeling its strange warmth. "If there's anything connecting the two of them, they already have that information."

"Don't you think—"

"I think that I need this book in order to help someone who's close to death." Emily stared at her colleagues, feeling like they were strangers. "Once it's served its purpose, I'm happy to take it directly to the police. I'm not sure Terrence will be happy about that since it implicates him in a burglary, but I'll let them decide how to treat the information. Until I've saved Sheryl Hawthorne, I'm not handing it to anyone."

Wanda clapped her hands. "You go, girl. Tell them how it is."

Emily tried to place the book in her bag, alongside the puzzle, but it was too large to fit. She lifted it up, hugging it tightly. "I'll bring it back tomorrow at the latest."

When she walked to the door, Pete hovered but didn't stop her leaving. Emily kept her head down as she got into her car, only then looking around her before placing the precious volume on the passenger seat.

"Don't crash, whatever you do," Wanda warned her. "That's how this entire mess got started."

"I'll be careful. Where do I need to go now? Do I take it to the hospital?"

When Wanda didn't immediately answer, Emily shot her a sidelong glance. The ghost witch was chewing on her bottom lip, staring at her hands.

"What is it?"

"You'll need someone to help you out. Usually, it wouldn't matter but with my sister unable to participate, someone needs to hold the book and recite the spell, while another aligns the puzzle to set her soul free."

"Sounds like voodoo to me."

Wanda turned a furious glare on Cynthia. "That's because you have no respect for things outside of what you see and hear. I bet you didn't believe you were a ghost until someone proved it to you!"

Emily sniggered inwardly, remembering exactly the struggle she'd gone through. "Harvey will be the best shot. He already knows more about you two than I'd like."

Luckily, this time Harvey was home. Emily had just started to explain his help was required when her phone beeped.

"Invoice attached. I reduced the total due to the latest developments. I'm so sorry," the robotic voice relayed.

Emily frowned and passed the phone across to Harvey for inspection.

"It's a lawyer named Gareth. He's billed you one dollar," he said, flipping back to the home screen. "Oh, no."

"What is it?"

"There's been a court order issued." Harvey gave her a look so dripping with sympathy that Emily wanted to slap him. "They've agreed to withdraw life support from Sheryl Hawthorne. They've unplugged her machines today."

CHAPTER TWENTY-TWO

You were too slow.

Emily staggered backwards, her legs giving way. She cast her arm out to try to catch herself but only managed to crack her knuckles on the dining table. The spell book—the thing she'd fought so hard to find—slid out of her grasp.

"Sis, are you all right?"

Harvey swam in and out of focus. A pulse beat through Emily's head, far too consuming to focus on anything else.

This is it. The bone fragments have slipped. You're dying.

Her brother's hand grabbed hold of her shoulder but the only sensation she recorded was pressure. He might as well have been touching somebody else.

"Snap out of it, Scarface. I don't mind you on occasion but it's far too early to put up with you twenty-four seven."

As though a bucket of ice water had been thrown in her face, Emily snapped out of her shock. She sat up, pressing a hand to her chest as her heart stuttered, then returned to its usual steady beat. The book lay awkwardly underneath her leg, a bruise where she'd fallen on top of it already forming.

"Stay down. I'm calling an ambulance."

"Don't," Emily called out, trying to catch the phone out of Harvey's hand.

He jerked away, out of reach, but his thumb stopped pressing the keypad. His right eyebrow arched up, nearly disappearing into his hairline. "Are you sure?"

"Of course, I'm sure. I feel foolish enough about fainting without calling in the cavalry to witness my shame." Emily brushed down her skirt and pulled the book out to one side. "Just give me a minute to catch my breath."

"I'll get the car out, then. We need to go to the hospital."

"It's already out." Emily waved a hand towards the driveway. "And I was just picking you up to take you there."

Except it doesn't matter now.

A wave of tears overwhelmed her, and Emily buried her face in her hands. She couldn't bring herself to glance at Wanda. Her emotions were raw—they wouldn't be able to absorb the ghost's on top of them.

"I have to go," Wanda said, her voice a thin shadow of itself. "I need to check."

"No, you don't." Cynthia sounded as firm as a nineteen-fifties school ma'am. "You stay here, Witchy-poo and keep Scarface company. I'll be back in a jiffy."

"Don't stand up!" Harvey yelled as Emily struggled to her feet.

When she managed to stand unaided, he hovered around her, his hands opened to catch her if she fell.

"I know it's an awful shock," he said, checking the phone message again. "But the court wouldn't have made the decision if they didn't think it was the right one."

"That's rubbish!" Wanda shook her head, her voice gaining in volume and strength. "They've been hoodwinked by the Supreme. Just like she once tried to get the better of Sheryl and me."

"Try to think of the people whose lives will be saved because of her generosity as an organ donor," Harvey continued. "There'll be people who can see, and breathe, and... and..."

"Filter waste through their kidneys?" Emily suggested.

"You can't give up on her. There's still a chance." Wanda spun around, her arms open. "If you speed to the hospital, you might get there in time."

"What time was the message sent?" she asked Harvey. "The original one to Gareth, not his to me."

"At eleven o'clock," he said, his face a study in misery.

"That's just an hour after we left the courtroom," Emily said, biting her lip when the world wavered in front of her again. "The judge must have considered the application as his next case."

The tears came again, and Emily gave in to the wrenching sobs. Ugly crying. She didn't care who saw.

"Perhaps you should lie down," Harvey suggested. "What have you had to eat today?"

"I don't remember." Emily wiped the last of the tears away with the back of her hand, gratefully accepting Harvey's handkerchief when he handed it across to her. She blew her nose and inhaled a deep breath, releasing it slowly. "I might go to bed for a while. If I'm not up by six o'clock, would you come and wake me?"

Harvey nodded, again following her with his hands spread like a catcher's mitt until she was safely in her bedroom. Wanda stood at the end of the bed, but Emily still couldn't look at her. She didn't have anything to say.

"Hey," she called out just as her brother left the room. "Did Dad ever say what happens when you're not able to help a ghost out with their plight?"

He jerked his face away, but not quickly enough for Emily to miss the look of fear written on it. "I don't know. He never said."

She lay on the bedspread, closing her eyes. She could chase him up for the truth later if it even mattered. Whatever the answer to her question, she'd know it soon enough, first hand.

"Could you wait out in the lounge?" Emily asked the room, not bothering to open her eyes to see if Wanda still stood there. "I'd just like to be by myself for a minute. Once I've had a nap, we can sort out what comes next."

After a minute passed with no reply, she cracked open an eyelid and breathed a sigh of relief to find the room empty. Her phone beeped again, and she half thought about turning it off, but in the end, played out the message after reducing the volume.

"You don't really know me," the phone recited, "but it's Terrence Salem and I need your help. I've left a special book upstairs in your charity shop and I want you to bring it to me. I think you know what it's for."

He recited an address, a street and number Emily didn't know, then the message continued, "Please don't tell my sister, Agnetha. This is nothing to do with her."

Emily's eyes flicked open, and she stared up at the ceiling.

She might have lost her chance to help Sheryl Hawthorne, but she could still help herself. If Agnetha could really remove the scars from her accident, here was her chance.

Please don't tell my sister...

But, as Terrence had pointed out, Emily didn't know him. What did she care what his wishes were?

EMILY'S MIND was chasing itself in circles when Cynthia announced her presence with a harsh cough.

"Oh, good. You're awake. I can't say the same thing about Sheryl, but she's certainly not dead."

Emily sat upright, a quick gaze confirming Wanda wasn't there. "Why not?"

"Don't sound so upset, I thought it was good news. As far as I can see, the hospital hasn't got around to switching anything off. I don't know why. Perhaps the court changed its mind again."

With a frown, Emily picked up her phone and saw a new message. She asked it to play.

"Sergeant Winchester here. The young woman you revived is being withdrawn from life support tonight, at eight o'clock. They're waiting until everyone who wants to has the chance to say goodbye. I thought you might want to know."

"What's that?" Wanda hovered in the doorway, half in and half out of the room. "Sheryl's still alive?"

"She is until eight this evening." Emily struggled to her feet, wiping her hands over a face still swollen from crying. "How long will the ceremony take?" She glanced around the room, her stomach lurching when she didn't see the spell book.

Cynthia gave a chuckle. "It's in the other room, Scarface. Don't have another attack."

"It won't take more than an hour," Wanda said with a beaming smile which then faltered. "You'll just need a bit of time to sort out all the Latin."

"The what?" Emily stared at her in confusion. "You never mentioned..."

"It's in the book," Wanda interrupted. "It's all laid out, simple enough for anyone to recite aloud."

"Anyone who can read, you mean," Cynthia said with a little snigger. "You really got the wrong woman for this task."

"Harvey? What's the time?"

Her brother came to the door, frowning as he saw her brushing her hair. "It's ten to six. I was just about to call you."

"We need to get to the hospital, right now," Emily said. She tilted her head back, letting her fingertips feel their way along her unsightly scar. The thought of contacting Agnetha about Terrence could wait. First, she needed to do everything in her power to save Sheryl.

"Are you feeling worse?"

As Harvey's face filled with alarm, Emily realised she should explain a few things. "Don't worry. I'm fine. In fact, I'll drive. According to an expert, I need you to read through a spell written in a foreign language. It'll take a while to sort out how to say it."

Although he followed her out the door willingly enough, taking hold of the spell book with something akin to reverence, Harvey frowned. "What are you talking about? Why are we going to the hospital?"

"It's nothing to worry about," Emily reassured him. "We just need to kidnap a patient then perform some ancient ritual over her. I've been told it won't take much longer than an hour!"

CHAPTER TWENTY-THREE

Deciding that any extra help would come in handy, Emily directed Harvey to pick up Crystal on the way. She was just finishing up with a client and with Emily's assistance got them out of her parlour in a few seconds flat.

"I can't believe you finally got everything," Wanda said, her voice a mixture of excitement, relief, and intense worry. "Once you recite the spell, my sister's spirit should fly out of the puzzle box and turn her back into a full human being."

"Why do you need to kidnap Sheryl?" Crystal asked after Emily filled her in on what was happening.

"Because we don't need the hospital turning her off, mid-sentence. It'll be better if we can take her off-site."

Harvey was pouring over the instructions and suddenly reached out a hand to grip Emily's upper arm. The car swerved. Three living passengers drew in a sudden breath.

"How about you just talk rather than grabbing me?"

"Sorry, it's just... You know you can't actually kidnap her from the hospital, right? I mean, if the machines are the things keeping Sheryl alive right now, removing her from them will have the same effect as the court order."

"Oh," Emily said in a small voice. "I should've worked that out for myself, shouldn't I?"

"What's that?" Crystal asked, leaning forward. "Is there a change of plan?"

When Emily repeated the problem, Crystal nodded. "What you actually need is someone to provide a big distraction. Long enough to keep everyone's mind on other things."

"Or," Harvey suggested, his voice hesitant, "we could just move her to a different room. While the hospital is sorting out its red tape, we could plug her back in somewhere else."

"Would that work?" Crystal asked. "What happens if the machines just reset themselves when they're unplugged."

Emily thought back to her overly long hospital stay. They were well out of the time period when earthquakes had rattled Christchurch and caused power surges and dips but the rebuild hadn't been beyond the protection of a crew digging through the wrong part of the road.

"They should have a memory. Long enough for a hospital to switch from mains power to its back-up generator."

"What's the worst that can happen?" Cynthia said in an amused tone. "You'll turn her off and Sheryl will die? Because that's what'll happen if you do nothing."

Emily nodded, her determination returning. "Right. We just have to hope it all keeps going long enough to swap Sheryl into a different room. Cynthia, you've been at the hospital, where's a place we can move her?"

"Just a minute." Harvey held his hand up as they pulled up near the market garden. "I think you're forgetting there'll be staff there. It's not as though you can just wheel a patient through the corridors without someone spotting it. You are moving an entire bed."

"How about we just get there and sort it out later?" Wanda cried. "We're wasting time."

"It's not a waste of time," Emily chastised her. "We'll still get to the hospital at the same time, whether we talk it all out during the journey or not."

Harvey and Crystal stared at her in amazement, privy to only one side of the conversation.

"Well, that's got her told," her brother said with a small laugh.

"I think we've been looking at this from the wrong side," Crystal said, snapping her fingers. "We're trying to keep Sheryl out of the reach of the hospital staff, right?"

"Right," the carful chorused back.

"Then we should kidnap the staff on duty. If we bung up the lift by pressing the emergency bell and put a broom handle or something through the doors from the stairwell, we'll only be dealing with a few staff members, won't we?"

"Cynthia?" Emily asked, giving her a quick glance over her shoulder.

"On it," the ghost said, disappearing.

"This all sounds like a disaster waiting to happen," Harvey said.

When Emily flicked her eyes towards him in concern, her brother seemed to be enjoying himself more than she'd seen him so far. "I don't suppose you have a few friends you can call as a back-up?"

"If you think it'll help," he replied earnestly, pulling his phone out of his pocket.

"Oh, my goodness." Emily wanted to slap her forehead, only stopping because she still had to hold on to the wheel to drive.

"What?" Crystal and Harvey sang out.

"I know the perfect people for the task and they're already in Christchurch." She fumbled for her phone and passed it back to Crystal. "Call up the number under Slim and Co. Ask him if he could get the entire gang to the back entrance of the hospital by seven at the latest."

"You think we'll make it by then?" Harvey said, looking up from the spell book long enough to glance at the clock.

"Until somebody proves it otherwise."

Emily kept her eyes steady on the road, easing her speed as high as she dared. With her attention focused, she missed most of the phone call to the Mortal Guises, but Crystal nodded as she finished. "They'll be there. Now we just need to meet them in one piece!"

"You're sure you'll be okay, reading out the spell aloud?" Emily asked, falling into the familiar pattern of nervousness —checking and rechecking.

"I'm sure."

Cynthia came back into the car, appearing glum. "There's five nurses on duty for the ward, plus a porter. There's no way we can take care of all of them."

Emily relayed the information to the car before filling the ghost in on the new additions to their plan. "We'll be fine. Even if it's just Slim and Pig who comes along, they'll be able to handle a bunch of nurses."

"It's a lot more than those two," Crystal said, staring wide-eyed around the car since she didn't know where the ghost was to address. "Slim promised us everyone on the ground at gang headquarters, at least a dozen."

"Is it just me, or does this sound like we're developing a solid plan?" Emily asked the car at large, tossing a wink towards Wanda. "I mean, we'll all end up in jail for a million years when this is over, but for the moment it feels pretty fantastic."

"There're still so many things that can go wrong," Wanda said, wringing her hands together.

"Why don't you concentrate on summoning up some sparks you had on hand the last time we visited the hospital?" After a second without any reaction, Emily added,

"Unless you think it's not worth Cynthia learning your secrets."

"Oh, yes." The ghost's eyes sparkled, and she clapped. "Come on, Witchy-poo. Give it up for Sheryl's sake."

"You know," Harvey mused as he closed the spell book. "It'll be nice when this is all over and you go back to only talking to people that I can see as well."

"Look out!"

With Wanda, Cynthia, and Crystal all screaming the same command at the same time, Emily's head nearly exploded. Her foot was pumping on the brakes before she recognised the figure standing in the middle of the road.

Agnetha. Dressed in full ceremonial robes.

She threw a bolt of electricity at the car and it flashed on the bonnet, making it impossible for Emily to see the road ahead. In a few steps, she wrenched the door open even as the car continued to move.

"Did you really think I'd let you get to the hospital and wake-up that traitor? It's not going to be that easy!"

CHAPTER TWENTY-FOUR

As Emily fumbled with her seat belt, the air inside the car shimmered, growing steadily hotter. She pushed against the door, tumbling out to land at Agnetha's feet.

"I told you not to mess in matters of life and death," the Supreme cried, flicking her hand to crack the air like thunder. "Did you think you could just go against my wishes? Since you don't want to take advantage of my generosity, I'm happy to put a stop to you right here."

Another crack, this time lightning scarring the night sky. Emily fell backwards, scrambling to crawl away with arms and legs too terrified to move.

"No, wait." Harvey's voice sounded far away.

When she flicked her eyes in his direction, he moved slowly, his limbs as wobbly and untrustworthy as hers.

"Leave her alone." Cynthia walked straight up to the Supreme, anger written large across her face. "That's my friend you're hurting."

"Ugh. A dead thing." Agnetha flicked a finger and Cynthia went flying. "You have to watch out for those. The dead bugs are the worst."

A flash of electricity hit the Supreme in the middle of her chest, throwing her backwards. Wanda stood beside the car, her arms raised to either side, energy crackling in the surrounding air.

"Finally got your powers in, did you?" Agnetha rubbed at the skin between her breasts, snarling. "Left it a bit late, I'm afraid."

She sent her own bolt of lightning towards Wanda. The ghost stared down in surprise as it tore through her body, then laughed as her ethereal flesh mended itself together.

"You'll have to do better than that." Wanda sent another bolt of electricity zinging from her fingertips. "We might be dead but you're a fool if you don't think that can be an advantage."

Emily took advantage of the fight to struggle to her feet, racing back to the car to help Harvey and Crystal out of the vehicle. The three of them stood there, awed by the display of power playing out in front of them.

"I've called the police," Crystal yelled out as Agnetha sent another bolt Wanda's way. "They'll be here soon. If you hurt any of us, we'll press charges."

The threat, usually such a large one with serious ramifications, just made the Supreme laugh. "Are you kidding me? You think Sergeant Winchester can put on handcuffs and make this go away."

She sent a fiery wave towards Crystal, driving her backwards with such force that her body thumped against the side of the car. When the force lessened, the medium staggered two steps forward, revealing a large dent in the metal panel.

"What do you want?" Emily called out. "We've done nothing to hurt you."

"I only want to watch you squirm in pain before you die," Agnetha yelled, panting at her exertions.

Wanda tackled her, perhaps forgetting she had little physical substance in the heady rush of her newfound power. As she spilled onto the ground beyond Agnetha, the Supreme laughed with surprised joy.

"No wonder my sister hated you," Wanda called out. "She couldn't wait to get out from under your so-called care."

"The feeling was mutual."

"Was it?" Wanda slowly got to her feet. "I seem to remember you crying for her to come home."

"Only until I realised she'd got Terrence under her thumb. I'd grown used to you and your sister's ingratitude but to take advantage of my brother like that…?" Agnetha's face twisted in disgust. "Your sister was worse than every evil creature in Pinetar!"

Crystal tugged at Emily's sleeve, pulling her back towards the car. Under her breath, she whispered, "We should try to make a break for it while she's otherwise occupied. Do you have the keys, or did you leave them in the car?"

At the sound, Harvey glanced over at the medium. "She sent a bolt of lightning racing towards the car a few minutes ago. I don't think you're going to escape her by having her look the other way."

The air crackled again as Agnetha sent a cloud of electricity towards her foe. Wanda danced like a marionette for a few seconds before she shook the effects off.

"It's hard to kill smoke," she taunted. "It doesn't matter that you've desperately held onto the position of supreme."

Agnetha threw back her head and roared at the sky. Rain clouds gathered, flooding the area with a rush of water more like a rising tide than a storm.

"What?" Wanda called out, openly mocking. "Do you believe that ghosts can't float?" She rose above the level of the rising water, shimmering with a brilliant light.

"Ungrateful. Little. Brat." With each word, Agnetha sent

another stream of electricity towards the ghost. Emily saw Wanda wince at the last one as though it had struck a physical blow.

"She's figuring out how to hurt her," she whispered to Crystal. "We need to distract her attention before she works it all out."

Without waiting to see if her friend understood, Emily stepped forward, holding her arms up to her side to appear bigger. "Are you so pathetic you can only play games with Caspar the ghost? Why don't you pick on somebody your own size?"

Agnetha turned, eyebrows raised in surprise, then burst into laughter. "What do you think *you're* going to do? Psychic me to death? Your powers don't scare me, darling. In case you haven't worked it out, I can see the dead, too."

"I can do more than that!" Emily put her hands on her hips, then threw back her head and laughed.

"What are you doing?" Harvey asked, bewildered.

Cynthia stepped forward, standing beside Emily and facing Agnetha with her trademark scorn. "Is this seriously all a Supreme can do? Here I was thinking it would be cool to have some powers. A bit of rain and a few lightning strikes might have impressed some villagers back in the dark ages but now? You're aware we've had special effects for quite some time?"

Agnetha strode towards the group. "This isn't some made-up light show. If I throw a bolt of electricity at your friend, it'll kill her." She panted and favoured her left side as she walked closer. Emily narrowed her eyes, recognising the signs of impending exhaustion.

"Someone threw a car at my sister once," Harvey yelled out, joining in their line-up. "It didn't cause more than a little scratch."

"It did a fair sight more than that." Agnetha advanced on

Emily, her upper lip curling. "You mightn't have realised since you've been gone so long, but your sister isn't quite in the land of the living right now." She poked a finger into the centre of Emily's chest. "You can practically smell the death coming off her. Pretty soon, she'll be as dead as your mum and dad."

"It's just a distraction," Cynthia said in a modulated tone. "Don't listen to her. She must be weaker than I thought to bother with underhanded tactics like this. What do you think, Wanda? Should we take her out?"

A bolt hit Agnetha square in the back, followed by a trilling giggle. "Bullseye!"

Her phone buzzed in Emily's pocket and she pulled it out, showing the screen to Harvey.

He read it and glanced at her, despair written across his face. "It's the police again. A text telling you if you want to say goodbye to Sheryl, you'd better hurry. They're switching the machines off in the next few minutes."

As Agnetha toyed with Wanda, getting her retribution for the latest attack, Emily could feel the seconds draining away. Soon, it wouldn't matter if they bested the Supreme or not. Sheryl only had one shot, then she'd be gone.

"Cynthia, can you get to the hospital? Throw a couple of IVs at the wall or something? Anything you can think of to give us a stay of execution."

"I'm not leaving you." The ghost's eyes were huge, her arms folded in a defiant line. "You must be crazy. We don't even know if the spell will work. Wanda could be fooling herself and you know it."

"She's the only reason we're out here. If Sheryl didn't matter, do you really think Agnetha would be doing this?"

"Sorry if I don't think Wanda's sister is worth losing my only friend!"

They glared at each other, the fight going on behind them

temporarily forgotten in their battle of wills. Finally, Emily smiled. "I'm your only friend?"

"Shut up." Cynthia turned away and looked up the road where a car with a souped-up engine was approaching. "Is that vehicle slowing down?"

"Bad luck if they think this is a rest area."

Even Agnetha seemed to realise something wasn't right. She'd been trying to strike Wanda with her magic force as the ghost hovered above her like an angel. Now, her attention focused on the approaching car, a look of absolute fury twisting her face.

"Jake!"

Their small group was forgotten as Agnetha stormed towards the road, flapping her arms to cause a cloud of mud and branches to float before her.

"What have you done with my brother?"

The car slowed to a halt, the lights still turned to high-beam, blinding the crowd that stood there. Even Agnetha raised a hand to shield her eyes, the mud cloud slumping to the ground with a wet thud.

A car door slammed, and a strange figure emerged. Emily's mind tried to resolve it into human form, this thing with four arms, four legs, and two heads.

Two people.

Jake the Snake bared his teeth at Agnetha as he approached, holding Terrence in an arm-lock.

"Remember our agreement, Aggie? The one you broke when you robbed me of the book I needed?" He twisted his hand, revealing the long blade he was holding tightly up to Terrence's throat. "I think it's time to renegotiate."

CHAPTER TWENTY-FIVE

As Emily stared at Jake, pieces of the puzzle she'd been chasing for the past few days began to slot into place. "You sent the message," she said, wanting to step towards him but scared it would place Terrence in more jeopardy. "You pretended to be Terrence."

Jake laughed. "After going to so much trouble to locate the spell book, I was hardly going to let it go to waste. You should have answered me." He spat in the ground and snarled at Agnetha. "This one was never going to help you out. She can't even cast a proper love spell."

Wanda's mouth fell open and she switched her gaze from Jake to Emily in disbelief.

"How much did you hate that Sheryl genuinely fell in love with Terrence?" Emily took a step forward, keeping watch on the position of the knife from the corner of her eyes. "The only way you could get her attention was by forcing her."

"But that's—" Wanda swallowed and shot a glance full of daggers at Agnetha. "That's against the coven rules, not to mention the law."

"I think Agnetha's been doing a lot of things against the

law," Emily said. "What did she promise you, Jake? That if you worked together to get hold of the spell book and puzzle, Sheryl could be all yours? When did you work out you couldn't trust her?"

"She didn't want you." Wanda raised her hand to her forehead, rubbing hard. "That's why we let the rent run through on our flat. That's why we were headed out of town, to check out houses in Christchurch."

The scales fell from Emily's eyes. "You ran them off the road. Of course! That's why you've got the burn marks up half your arm. Sheryl tried to run away and you're so shallow and nasty you wouldn't let her go. You'd rather she died than be with the man she truly loved. At least you and Agnetha had that in common."

"Stop it!" Jake turned, dragging Terrence with him to face Agnetha, Wanda, and Emily in turn. "I want the spell book and the puzzle. If you don't give them to me, I'm killing Terrence right here and now."

"No!" Agnetha stepped forward, holding her hands out and shaking. "Please. I'll make it right with you. Just let my brother go."

"Why isn't she sending a bolt to kill him?" Cynthia whispered to Wanda. Emily saw the problem as soon as she asked. Jake held Terrence in such a tight grip that if Agnetha hit one, she'd hit both.

"I don't believe you," Jake shouted back at Agnetha. "You sent someone in to steal from me after we made our agreement. Do you take me for a fool?"

"It was Belinda." Emily glanced at Terrence who gave the faintest nod. "She stole the book."

Jake growled and span to face her. "Who the hell is that?"

"No, she didn't." Agnetha stared in confusion at Emily. With fear morphing her face, she didn't look like the Supreme any longer. She was a scared old woman.

Well, join the club.

"Honestly, Jake. All I did was ask Belinda to check and see you really had the book. With the mix-up over the puzzle, I needed to make sure you were telling me the truth, but she couldn't find it." Agnetha still held her hands out in a placating gesture but her lip curled. "You were the one lying to me!"

Emily thought of what the redhead had told her. A lie. It had been so quick, she should have realised its basis was in truth. But it wasn't Agnetha that Belinda had been pounding on the door, demanding to see. It was Terrence.

She'd worked as a double agent. Telling Agnetha the book was gone as she handed it to Terrence.

Jake dug the tip of his knife a little deeper, drawing blood. "Why did you go after the puzzle box, then? That was when I really understood what you were up to. If you didn't want to restore Sheryl as a treat for your little brother, why did you burgle her house?" He jerked his chin at Emily.

"I didn't. It was just some weird story she told the police."

"It was obviously Terrence, you dolt. Like it matters!" Wanda thundered. "Even if you revived my sister, she's certainly not going to spend the rest of her days with you."

But Jake couldn't hear the ghost's protests.

Emily stamped her foot in frustration. "Sheryl was never going to choose you. Not after you ran her off the road. You killed her sister. You put her in a coma and thanks to this one"—she flapped a hand at Agnetha—"her machines are about to be turned off."

Jake's mouth fell open. "What?"

Agnetha's eyes opened wide. "No, it's a mistake. I was just trying to—"

"It's a mistake that just cost your brother his life." Jake tightened the muscles of his arm, shifting his grip on the knife.

"It's too hot for you to hold." Wanda moved close to Jake and stared at his face. He winced away, eyes flicking to and fro, able to sense her presence but unable to see her. "The knife blade is on fire. It's burning through the handle."

Jake cried out and dropped the weapon, at the same time tightening his hold on Terrence's neck. "Who did that?"

Agnetha was shaking so hard from fear, she dropped to her knees. "I swear, I had nothing to do with it. Please, let my brother go."

Wanda glanced over to Cynthia and winked. She sent out a curving line of electricity, zapping along the knife's edge, then whipping it back and into her hand.

"What's happening?" Jake's voice moved into a register so high, only dogs and children could hear it. "I'll hurt Terrence if you do anything else."

"Please, Wanda. Stop now. We can talk it out." Agnetha tried to scramble to her feet but slipped in the mud. "Don't let my brother get hurt."

The ghost shook her head. "I'd care about that statement if you hadn't signed a death warrant on my sister." She lifted the knife up, using the electricity as a substitute for a physical body. Jake stared at the weapon, entranced.

Emily remembered what Pete and Gregory had told her—Terrence liked to take risks. With Jake's focus temporarily elsewhere, she gave the captive man a nod, and he drove his elbow hard into his captor's belly.

As Jake bent double, he loosened his grip enough for Terrence to spin free of his grasp. A few more steps and he'd danced out of harm's way.

"Don't kill Jake," Cynthia called out to Wanda and Emily turned to her in surprise. "You don't want to have his wretched personality filling up the afterlife a second before it has to."

Wanda laughed once, then threw the knife in a curving

parabola, slicing through the air. Its handle landed with a meaty thump on Jake's forehead, leaving a dent, and she pulled it back to her.

As the man's eyes rolled up into his head and his knees sagged, she sent the blade careening through the air again. It landed, another bullseye, digging into the thick denim at Jake's crotch and skewering him to the ground.

"Ouch," Harvey said, wincing, and Emily wondered at the capacity of men to feel for each other, even when one of them was a maniac.

"Don't worry," she called out, relaying Wanda's explanation. "It didn't get him anywhere that'll leave a scar." She moved over and checked Jake's blank face. "It looks like it's knocked him out cold, though."

"Come here," Agnetha called, holding her arms open for Terrence to run into.

Instead, he scowled and shook his head. "You killed my girlfriend."

"It was for your own good."

A light split open the air behind Wanda, glowing with an intensity that was hard to look at for long. Emily shielded her eyes, recognising the doorway. Crystal gasped in wonder, also having seen it before.

"What's going on?" Wanda stared at the opening as though it was a gateway to hell.

Cynthia grabbed her by the elbow and dragged her forward. "Time to go, Witchy-poo."

"But my sister!"

"She'll be following you along soon enough if she isn't there already." Mrs Pettigrew stamped her foot when Wanda continued to resist. "You can't ignore the doorway. This isn't something that goes away."

"But—"

"We tracked down your killer," Emily said, her voice low.

"It must be the reason you were still here, even if you thought it was to save your sister. I'm sorry." She reached out, feeling her heart leap from the comfort of Harvey sliding his fingers into her hand.

"I can't go." Tears streamed down Wanda's face. "Sheryl needs me."

"Judging from the figures I can see moving about in there, she's already waiting for you." Cynthia's voice was the kindest Emily had heard from the woman. Even though she didn't understand the reasoning behind the pool of light—if there was reason to be had in something so mysterious—she believed it must be a sign for her witchy companion to go.

"You can come back if you need to," she called out. "Cynthia can show you how."

"Just as soon as you show me your other tricks," Mrs Pettigrew agreed, taking a firmer grip on Wanda's arm and dragging her farther into the glowing light.

Emily had to turn away as it grew even brighter. Tears fell from her eyes, from the brightness, from the sorrow. The doorway to another realm might have appeared, but she had most certainly failed.

"Well," Agnetha clapped her hands together. "Wasn't that a lovely ending? Now, Terrence, I can't offer you a lift home but I'm hoping Jake won't mind if we steal his car."

"I told you I wasn't going anywhere with you." Terrence shook his head, staring at his sister in disbelief. "After everything you've done, how can you believe that I'd come home and live with you." He swallowed, his voice thicker than usual. "You've killed the only woman I've ever loved."

Agnetha's smile stayed in place for a full minute. When it caved, it did so in degrees, leaving her eyes, her cheeks, her lips, leaving only a mask of rage.

"You'll do what I tell you, young man. Our parents left me in charge of your welfare and like it or not, I'm looking out for you. Now get into Jake's car before I have to force you. I don't want you to appear like a spoiled brat in front of such low company."

When he still didn't move, she forced a calm expression onto her face.

"Come on now, Terrence. Remember what fun we used to have when you were little. We'd play battleships or hide and seek. It can all be like that again."

"You. Killed. My. Girlfriend."

"She wasn't your girlfriend. She was an ungrateful brat who never had the decency to thank me for everything I did for her. Sheryl might have twisted you around her little finger with her flattery and her curves but it's all a lie. She dropped you like a hot potato the first time Jake showed an interest."

"You put her under a compulsion." Terrence walked up to his sister and pointed his finger into her face. "That's the only reason she turned away from me. Even then, even with all your powers as Supreme, you couldn't keep the charade up. When that idiot drove her off the road, she was driving to be with me!"

"I've done everything in my life to protect you and this isn't any different. She's a dirty girl. She wasn't fit to be your partner. You should drop down onto your knees and thank me for looking out for you. Can you imagine what life would be like if you'd knocked her up?"

"Heaven." Terrence's voice broke. "It would have been heaven. I've never felt so blessed as in the time I spend with Sheryl. I don't care what your opinion is of her—I've never sought your counsel and I never will."

"Do what I say!" Agnetha sent a bolt of lightning spiralling out of her fist. It headed straight for Terrence's face, then at the last moment, diverted and hit the ground near Jake's head.

"I would rather die than spend another minute in your company."

Agnetha gnashed her teeth, frustration spilling out of her as pure static energy. "Fine," she shouted. "If you want to die, I'll take everyone out here along as a favour. Is that what you want?"

Emily held her breath, her body turning to ice as she watched Terrence nod. The light behind her was fading away, closing up the entrance between worlds. Leaving her stuck in the land of the living with a madwoman.

With a gasp, Emily pulled her hand out of her brother's and leapt toward the shrinking door of light.

CHAPTER TWENTY-SIX

"You can't be here," Cynthia called out. She ran at Emily, trying to push her back but it was too late. The doorway sealed. The battle of sibling wills unfolding by the side of the road disappeared. "What have you done?"

"A small group can't defeat the Supreme's power. Not alone. We need your help."

Wanda stood, mouth open, a frown creasing her face. "But there's only us here. Even if we could go back, we've already tried and failed."

"You defeated Jake."

"I overpowered a talentless man. It's not a challenge."

Cynthia tugged at Emily's hand, her flesh as solid as Harvey's had been a minute earlier. "You must go back. If you stay here, you'll be as dead as us."

Emily planted her feet and stood her ground. "When I first talked to Agnetha, she told me since I could speak to the dead, I should be able to locate her brother easily. The dead are everywhere, she told me. I need their help now."

"In case you haven't noticed, there's just us here." Cynthia pulled at Emily's arm again, then dropped it in frustration when she refused to move. "Where's this dead army you think exists? Do you see them?"

"I could never see any of you until an accident scarred my brain. Does that mean you didn't exist?"

"Great. You're speaking in riddles. What I know is that if you don't stay in the realm of the living, you're dead."

"Then I'll be dead. It hasn't harmed you any." Emily tried to look around her but there was nothing but brilliant white light in every direction. With every second, even Wanda and Cynthia faded, absorbed into the radiance. She didn't have much time.

Do I really believe the dead are everywhere? Yes. Yes, I do.

Emily put her hands over her abdomen, filling her lungs up from the base as a long-ago speech instructor had taught her to do. "I need your help. Every dead person who has a connection to Pinetar, I call upon you for assistance. A madwoman has taken up the mantle of Supreme and is not fit for the role."

Wanda had gone. Nothing but white was in her place. Cynthia barely existed.

"My father passed a gift down to me but it's only recently I've begun to use it. I've had no instruction so I must work from instinct. My belief is that I must now reach out to you."

A shape wavered in the unending brightness. The outline of a person, so familiar, so long-ago left behind. A hand reached out to take hold of Emily and draw her close, into a hug.

"I am the father of Emily Curtis and I spent my life in service to this nation, just as she has begun to serve you now. I beseech you to join together with us, to fight against a powerful enemy."

Cynthia grabbed hold of Emily's arm, appearing in full

view with the blink of an eye. Wanda stood beside her, a row of people lining up as far as her vision now saw.

"We will come."

"Okay, it looks like there's something to this, Scarface. Lead us into battle."

Emily closed her eyes and felt along the love she held for her brother. She travelled its bends and curves until she could feel the cold of an earthly night.

Peanut ran in a figure eight around her ankles, mewing. She laughed and bent to lift him up to her shoulder. "Come along, then. We can lead the charge."

In a blink, Emily stood back on the side of the road. The burned and flooded vestiges of the destruction which Agnetha had so far brought to bare lay in every direction.

An argument played out in front of her, Terrence standing his ground.

"You're not thinking straight," Agnetha yelled at her brother.

Terrence flung his hands up into the air. "Of course, I'm not thinking straight. My girlfriend is dying in hospital today because of your actions." He glanced across at Emily who took a second to rally, part of her still existing in another realm. "I'm sorry I broke into your house. Did you ever find the book?"

She frowned, catching back up to speed with the scene playing out. "Yes, I found it. We were on our way to the hospital when your sister stopped us."

"They finally have the means to save Sheryl, and you stopped them? Are there any depths you won't sink to?"

"All I want is what's best for you. It's what any sister wants for her brother. Stop trying to take my love and twist it into something it's not."

"Love." Emily laughed, holding her brother's hand aloft.

"This is love. My brother moving home to care for me, even when I wouldn't admit I needed it. That's love." She took a step closer to the Supreme. "A dead woman trying desperately to stay in this realm to ensure her sister's safety. That's love."

"Wanting your brother to avoid making a mistake that will cost him pain and years of his life entangled with a woman who's wrong for him—that's love too."

"No, it's not." Terrence's whole body shook with the denial. "It's possessive. I'm not some figurine you can store on your mantelpiece. I'm a grown man, capable of making my own decisions."

"But they're bad. If you'd married Sheryl, your life would be terrible."

"So what? It's none of your business. If you really loved me, you'd stand back and let me fail. You'd let me do the things I'm good at and stop trying to fit me into a box that only comes in the wrong size."

Emily saw Agnetha drawing up her strength, her power. A middle-aged woman whose energy was flagging, but she was about to give her all in another attempt at destruction.

Well, two could play at that game.

Emily raised her hands up, turning towards the flickering crowd of the dead as though she was a conductor in front of her orchestra. Wanda tilted her head back, the energy thrumming down to fill her, straight out of the sky.

She dropped her hands, ready-set-GO! Wanda's energy passed through all the dead spirits, shooting spirals of electricity straight out of their chests. No, their hearts.

"It's really easy once you get the hang of it," Cynthia shouted, her face suffused with joy. She bore down, her sparks increasing in intensity.

Again, Emily raised her arms, and the crowd fell still and silent. Again, she dropped them, and the streams of electricity flowed out of the congregating spirits, converging on Agnetha.

"You're just dead bugs!" The Supreme flung her hands up to fight against the pulses heading towards her. "You should go back where you came from."

"Not unless we take you with us," Emily's father called out, her mother joining in with his cry a second later.

Next to her, Harvey raised his fists to the sky, shaking them in encouragement. The dead continued to pour forth from the other realm, spilling out until it seemed all of Pinetar's decedents must be standing there.

"Help." Collapsing under the onslaught, Agnetha stretched a hand out towards her brother.

Terrence stood firm, shaking his head. "Whatever you're suffering, you brought it upon yourself."

The electricity continued to flow towards the Supreme until it became a glowing ball equal in strength to the door the dead had come from. With a gigantic thunder of sound, it suddenly compressed to the size of a basketball, then a tennis ball, then a ball-bearing.

A whoomph and the electricity was gone. Agnetha dropped to the ground.

CHAPTER TWENTY-SEVEN

Emily stared at the rows of ghosts, unable to give voice to everything inside her heart. A tear dribbled down her cheek, but she couldn't raise her hand to brush it away. Her parents stood just metres away.

"Where did they all come from?"

She jerked around, staring at Crystal who was gazing at the crowd of the dead, her mouth agape.

"You can see them?"

"It would be hard not to. Barry!" Crystal ran, making for a large man standing near the edge of the group. Her hands travelled straight through his body, leaving her stumbling and laughing. "Are you really here?"

"It's good to see you kids helping each other out." Emily's dad stepped forward, nodding to her and Harvey. "For a long time there, we thought you'd never reconnect."

"Dad?" Harvey stretched his hand out, letting it brush through the side of their father's arm. "Mum?"

"I can't tell you how relieved I am that you're working together."

Emily moved a step forward as her mother spoke,

wishing she was on the other side of the light, so she could still connect to them physically. She'd never wanted anything more in her life than to give them a hug.

"We have to go." Her dad looked over his shoulder, brow darkening as he watched the vibrant glow of light begin to dim. "Can't get stuck over here. You've got quite enough on your plates without taking care of your parents, too."

Harvey grabbed hold of Emily's shoulders and they waved goodbye. Peanut scrabbled with his claws in the dirt, being dragged backwards by some invisible force until she bent and scooped him into her arms. "You can stay."

Cynthia and Wanda resisted the force of the door closing. "Are you sure you don't want to go back?" Emily asked the witch as she fought to hold her ground. "It mightn't open up for you again."

"I'm sure. No matter what the other realm holds, it doesn't have my sister. I need to stay here until I'm sure what happened to her."

"Ugh. Why is she still here?" Cynthia asked, pointing to the ground where Agnetha's body lay.

"Is she dead?" Emily walked over, picking up a stick on the way to give the body a poke. A reactive flinch told her otherwise. "Nope. Just unconscious."

"Her power is gone." Wanda stood nearby, cupping her elbows and staring at the collapsed woman with something akin to wonder. "The sheen she always had about her—it's left. She's no longer our Supreme."

"Well, thank goodness. She hardly seemed fit for the role." Crystal hooked her arm through Emily's, smiling at the ghost witch.

"You can still hear her?" Emily's mouth fell open.

"Loud and clear." Crystal broke away to give her body an urgent pat. "I hope that doesn't mean I'm dead."

"You're fine," Emily said with a smile. She poked her friend in the upper arm, dimpling the batwings there. "See?"

"Keep your fingers to yourself, hey? I didn't grow all this gloriousness"—she waved over her Rubenesque frame—"just for you to poke at."

"Should we tie her up while she's still out for the count?" Harvey peered at Agnetha, standing a respectable distance back. "And what's happening with Jake."

"Ugh. With what those two did to my sister, I hope they never wake up again."

Harvey gave Jake a kick, and the man groaned, then fell back into unconsciousness. "I don't think we need to worry about either of them for a while."

"Wait." Emily stared at Wanda in confusion. "What do you mean, your sister wasn't on the other side?"

"Oh." Crystal blushed, blood rushing to her face in a flood. "I might know what's going on there. In fact…" She clicked her fingers at Terrence who gave her a blank stare in return. "The phone?"

He handed it over, and Crystal scrolled through the messages. Emily had to bite her lip. The device was her lifeline and watching it in someone else's possession made her nervous, no matter how much she trusted them.

"While you were having a disagreement with Agnetha, your mate Slim sent a text through. His gang got to the hospital in record time, so I gave him a few instructions."

"What instructions?" Emily narrowed her eyes at the medium, who shrugged.

"I just laid out the plan as I understood it. At least, what we would've been doing if this maniac"—she jerked her chin toward Agnetha's supine body—"hadn't pulled us off to the side of the road."

Wanda stared, a slew of emotions racing across her

features. "You mean they subdued the staff and blocked off the floor?"

"Something like that. I'm a bit blurry on the details but I suggest we get down there now. From what Slim says, your sister is still plugged in and doing fine but they've got police camped outside along with a hostage negotiator."

"Oh, my." Emily pressed a hand to her chest, a smile blossoming on her face. "I really thought we'd missed the window of opportunity."

"Thank the Mortal Guises for the stay of execution." Crystal scurried for the car, slipping in the mud strewn about the place. "But if we don't get a move on, it'll be in vain. You've still got the book and the puzzle box, don't you?"

"I certainly do."

She reached for the driver's side door handle, but Harvey put a hand on her shoulder. "I don't think so. You and Crystal get in the back and be ready to jump out the moment the car comes to a stop. I'll deal with the police and you work out how to get inside."

"But I can't read—"

"I'll do the recitation. You handle the soul." Crystal winked at Wanda and Cynthia. "Come on, ladies. Let's get this done."

THERE WERE SO many police cars pulled up outside, Emily began to think their mission would be impossible. Close by the hospital entrance, an inspector stood with a loudspeaker. He barked out a few sentences, all of them illegible to her ears.

"Do you think we should slip around the back?"

"Come with me," Crystal said, pulling her out of the car.

While she stumbled along behind her friend, the medium squinted up the side of the building.

"They'll have disabled the lifts, so it's no use taking them. What we need to do is get into the stairwell, then text them when we're on the right floor."

"All of which is postponed until we actually get inside." Emily waved her hand at the line up of law enforcement. "No offence, but I think we might be outmanned."

"There's a staff door," Cynthia said, appearing out of nowhere as usual. Wanda trailed along behind her, face pinched with concern. "It's meant to be kept clear as an exit but there's a heap of cigarette butts telling me it's frequently used. That means it won't be alarmed."

"Can we open it from the outside, though?"

"I'll poltergeist it from the inside. Just move along the side of the building and around the corner."

Emily gripped her bag as she navigated down the dark alleyway. It would be too much irony to endure if she lost the puzzle box just as the plan was coming to fruition.

Crystal did the same with the book, curling both arms around it in a protective shield.

"Now wait out here," Cynthia directed, "and I'll go inside and push it open."

"Stand back." Wanda stepped forward, raising a hand. "I've got this."

With a bang, the door flew open and slammed against the wall, straining its hinges.

"Remind me not to get you in a bad mood," Crystal muttered as she passed through the entrance, her voice hushed with awe.

"It's just a party trick." Cynthia sniffed as she floated inside. Her obvious disgruntlement made Emily smile.

"These stairs are going to kill me," Emily said, loosening

one hand from its death grip on her handbag to clutch the handrail. "How much time do we have?"

"Just get up there and worry about the consequences in the morning." Cynthia stayed a few steps ahead, giving a come-on gesture as encouragement. "You've done worse. Since you handled a few minutes of compressions without falling apart, these stairs should be a doddle."

They weren't but Emily concentrated all her energy on getting up them. By the time they reached the third-floor level, her lungs had taken over as chief complainants.

"Give me the phone and I'll call Slim and the gang," Crystal said. Her words came between pants as well but of the two, she was slightly fitter.

A minute later, a sound of wrenching metal greeted them from the other side and Pig pulled open the stairwell door. "The police are going to town with the bribes," he said, staying behind to shove a metal crowbar back into place. "I reckon they're stalling to get their men into position. We won't have long."

Emily remembered the room from her earlier visit and hurried there as quickly as her legs could carry her. The sight of Sheryl hooked up to the implacable machines warmed her heart, where before it had been enough to make her blood run cold.

The woman was alive. That was all that mattered.

If the spell worked, she'd soon be a lot better off.

"You'll have to read it out," Emily told Crystal, nodding her head. "If I need to do something with the puzzle, let me know."

Crystal opened the book, flipping through the pages. "Put the box by her head," she ordered. "And no laughing at my pronunciation."

With a deep breath, she began.

"I DON'T THINK it's worked," Emily said, her voice half lost to a sob. They'd run through the spell, following the instructions with Wanda correcting them when they strayed. After the final words were spoken, the two women had bowed their heads and stepped back, waiting for the miracle.

Ten minutes later, nothing had changed.

"How long should it take?" Emily shot a nervous glance toward the corridor where the men from the Mortal Guises gang paced back and forth.

Wanda leaned over her sister, peering intently at the unconscious woman's face. "I don't know. I've never done anything like this before. Well..." Her voice faltered.

"Well, what?" Cynthia asked. Her tone was sharp, and Emily wondered if she was still feeling miffed about the staff exit door.

"I tried it on a bunny rabbit once. But it didn't really have a lot going on upstairs, to begin with."

Emily resisted the urge to roll her eyes. Cynthia had no such compunction.

"After all the struggle to get here, the least I expected was for her to gasp and sit up. That's what they do in all the movies, isn't it?"

Crystal slung an arm around Emily's waist and hugged her. "I promise, we'll stay here for as long as we can and recite that spell as many times as we need to."

Wanda reached out a shaking hand and let a tiny whisper of energy reach out to caress her sister's cheek.

Sheryl gasped and sat bolt upright.

CHAPTER TWENTY-EIGHT

"I've never come out here since the ceremony," Emily said, placing a bouquet on her parents shared crematorium plot. "I didn't think of myself as the sentimental type."

Harvey put an arm around her shoulders. "Nor me. It's funny what seeing someone again, just for a second, can do to your emotions. I must've dreamed about Mum and Dad more in this past week than I have in years."

The ceremonial gardens were in the first flush of autumn. The trees alternated between evergreen and deciduous with leaves showcasing all the colours of the rainbow.

Emily thought it was strange how dead things could be so beautiful. The mixture of yellows, browns, oranges and reds were as vibrant as any bunch of spring flowers yet heralded the opposite end of the life.

"If we hurry, we'll have time for a cup of tea before we need to meet the real estate agent." She smacked her lips, tea now being a code-word for Harvey's baking.

Her brother opened the passenger side door for her before moving around to the other side. He'd taken up the mantle of driver. Although Emily might protest at some time in the future—she'd lost enough skills without letting the ones she did have atrophy—for the time being it was nice to have someone else navigate.

"I hope the owner's willing to negotiate." Harvey frowned as he stopped at an intersection. "If they're set on their asking price, it just feels like I'm wasting everyone's time."

Emily opened her mouth to say something—words she'd practised every night for the past week—then gasped instead. "Is that Terrence at the doorway?"

She fumbled for the handle and climbed out of the car, not caring for her lack of grace. "Howdy, stranger," she called out, waving. "What are you doing back here?"

"It's where my house is, remember?" Terrence moved over to give Emily a kiss on each cheek. He mimicked the French style of greeting but rather than air-kissing, he landed those suckers hard enough to count.

"We saw it for sale," Emily said, laughing. "So, you're not going to get away with that for an explanation."

"I've got to clear everything up before the open days." Terrence rolled his eyes and stuck his thick tongue out. "At this rate, I'll be worked to death before we get halfway through the move to Christchurch."

"When are they discharging Sheryl?" Emily pulled a seat out at the dining table and hurried through to the kitchen to fetch the Afghan biscuits Harvey had baked the previous night. To her mixed surprise and shame, they were half gone. Eating in front of the television was a habit she really had to stop.

Terrence was halfway through a biscuit before he swallowed and answered the question. "Once she passes the physical fitness exam at the end of this week, they'll sign her out. If she doesn't pass, I think Sheryl will just walk out against all medical advice."

"She's been there long enough," Emily said with a firm nod of empathy. "Good on her if she does take a stand."

"Except it means I need to get everything ready." Terrence swallowed hard and screwed up his mouth. "I'm not sure anything will be where it needs to be."

"She's in physical recovery." Emily gave a chuckle. "I doubt she'll care if the house is a bit messy."

"If she's trying to use a wheelchair to get about for the first few weeks, she'll care. It could be even longer until her leg muscles are developed enough to support her weight."

Emily stroked the long muscles of her thighs as they twitched in sympathy. "As long as you're around to shift stuff when she yells at you, it won't matter."

Terrence rolled his eyes. "Wow. You make cohabitation sound so appealing."

"When it's the right person, it is." Emily smiled and leaned across the table to poke Harvey's arm.

"How's Agnetha doing?" her brother asked.

"Still no sign of brain activity." Terrence gave a large sigh and rubbed his temple. The hairs there were thinning, a sign he should probably lose that gesture from his repertoire. "The hospital has arranged a meeting later in the month. I guess, if there's no change, it'll be up to me and my parents to come to a decision."

When the dust had settled from the battle, Agnetha and Jake had both been left unconscious. Although Jake had rallied sooner than anyone would like, Terrence's sister hadn't been so lucky. As Sheryl was preparing to give up her residency of the hospital ward, Agnetha was taking her place.

"If you need the help of a lawyer, I know a good one. He'll be able to talk you through the entire process and offer support along the way."

Although the motion Gareth had drawn up for her had been overturned, and quickly, Emily believed Agnetha's powers had more to do with that than a lack of skill on his part. It might take some of the professional sting away if he could perform the same activity without any mystical intervention.

"Slim dropped by yesterday," Terrence said after a short pause. "He and the gang think the police have finally given up the chase."

Emily smiled in relief. "Thank goodness."

Once it became clear the spell had worked, and Sheryl was back in the land of the living, the trouble the group was facing for getting to that point moved to centre stage.

"I thought for sure the police would nab us as we left," Terrence said, rubbing the back of his neck. "Slim didn't even hesitate."

"I think he might be on far better acquaintance with the police than most people," Emily said, then blushed. She was also on a first-name basis with the local officers—hardly in a position to cast judgement on others.

On the night, they'd stacked a row of chairs near the windows where the gang members had been standing guard. With bedspreads on top, the mock-humans wouldn't stay undiscovered for long, but they'd hoped it would gain enough time to slip down the stairs and out the back to escape.

Slim and the rest of the Mortal Guises had the foresight to wear balaclavas when they stormed the nurse's station and locked the on-duty staff into a cleaner's closet. Although Emily hated to think how much fear they must have engendered in the innocent hospital workers, it didn't tip the scales far enough to regret saving Sheryl's life.

CCTV should have been more of a problem but luckily Wanda's talent with electricity wiped clean the recordings from the machine and the backup hard drive. The only car within spotting distance by the police was Emily's. Harvey was safe from accusation, driving it around the block until Crystal signalled him, mission accomplished.

Emily had chosen to stay at Sheryl's bedside. Somebody had to be there to help fashion the events of the night differently from the reality. She'd spent many hours in a police cell, both in Christchurch and back in Pinetar, explaining that she hadn't seen any police blocking the entrance. She'd come to visit, couldn't find any staff on hand, then Sheryl woke up—it's a miracle!

By the time Sergeant Winchester finished his last interview, he was so exasperated she'd almost laughed. Luckily, a bite on her bottom lip put a stop to that. She couldn't imagine the merriment would have been well received.

"I'm just glad Wanda was able to put her talents to good use," Emily said, smiling. "If we had to pin a crime on anybody, I'm happy it could be Jake."

As Wanda explained, it was a simple push technique to change the story coming out of someone's mouth. The trick wasn't the problem. What caused her many hours of worry was ensuring she was across all the interviews happening in all the police stations. In the first days after the event, she'd hopped between seven different rooms, managing to keep them all straight. That alone was a feat to be celebrated.

Despite Sergeant Winchester's misgivings, the official version of events on the record was that Jake had turned up at the hospital, manic, and locked all the staff into a room. Although the policemen who'd first attended the callout insisted they'd seen more than one figure in the windows on that floor, one by one they retracted those statements, something in their memories shifting to accept an alternative scenario.

With all the eye-witnesses eventually coming around to the same story, there was little the police could do but turn the evidence over to the prosecution. Jake the Snake was in custody, awaiting a hearing on his plea.

Wanda would have a few more trips to court in her future but given what the man had done to her sister with Agnetha's help, she was more than willing to do whatever it took.

"Oh. I almost forgot." Terrence pulled a puzzle box out of his jacket pocket. "Sheryl insisted I give this back to you. She said it's only fair since you paid good money for the thing."

Emily turned the wooden toy over in her hand, holding it up to catch the light. Nothing about it drew her attention now. If this was sitting at the auction house today, she wouldn't even look twice.

Still, it could sit on the mantelpiece. Maybe, one day, a visitor would take it down and ask for the story behind it.

"I should be heading off, now," Terrence said with reluctance in his voice. "Honestly, I don't know how the house managed to fill up with so much stuff. Sometimes I think there'll never be enough boxes to pack it all."

"Well, you know the charity shop accepts donations, twenty-four seven. I'm happy to come out to your home and help you sort your belongings if you're willing to gift us everything you don't want to keep."

"That's a good point. I'll keep it in mind."

As she and Harvey waved goodbye on the front step, her watch relayed the time.

"Goodness, we'd better get a move on. Bryant will wonder where on earth we are and sell the place to somebody else."

"He'll probably end up doing that anyway," Harvey said with a sigh. "I really can't scrape together all that much and without a permanent job, the bank isn't likely to lend me money."

"The job with Crystal might be short on hours at the

moment, but I'm certain it'll grow to a full-time role, soon enough."

Unlike Harvey, Crystal's brush with the ghostly population of Pinetar hadn't left her when the door between realms closed. Emily could no longer lay claim to being the only true medium in the township.

It was early days, but it seemed certain her mediumship business would continue to expand. She'd already enlisted Harvey to act as secretary. Not a job he'd been trained for but one he enjoyed.

"Even if it doesn't, I'm sure you'll find something to keep you occupied around here." Emily hooked her arm through his. "And I've been thinking, it's silly for us to maintain two houses if we're both planning on staying in Pinetar."

"What do you mean?"

Emily giggled at the worried expression on her brother's face. Harvey did always seem determined to look on the bad side of any situation.

Just like a big brother should.

"I mean, if we both like the house, then I'm quite happy to put mine on the market and share the cost with you. It'll be silly for you to try to find a flatmate or live forever on my couch when we can share a perfectly good home."

A wary smile crept across Harvey's face. "Are you sure? This is a big commitment, you know. If we have a gigantic falling out, we'll be stuck with each other until we can sell again."

"I don't think that'll happen, but if it does, I volunteer to paint a line down the middle of every room."

Harvey rolled his eyes. "We haven't even taken a look at the place and already you're redecorating."

Emily laughed, then pulled on her brother's arm to stop him. She looked him squarely in the face. "Would you like to buy a house together?"

When he nodded, she threw her arms around him in a tight hug. Colour spread up his cheeks, and he nudged her away.

"You'll ruin my reputation as a hard man if there's anyone watching."

She snorted in amusement and turned back to the path. "Reputation's nothing. Family is everything."

ALSO BY KATHERINE HAYTON

Downward Dog (Dog Yoga Mysteries)

Miss Hawthorne Sits for a Spell (Charity Shop Haunted Mystery)

Mr Wilmott Gets Old School (Charity Shop Haunted Mystery)

Mrs Pettigrew Sees a Ghost (Charity Shop Haunted Mystery)

A Bed for Suite Dreams (A Hotel Inspector Cozy Mystery)

A Stay With Reservations (A Hotel Inspector Cozy Mystery)

A Job of Inn Dependence (A Hotel Inspector Cozy Mystery)

The Double Dip (Honeybee Cozy Mystery)

The Honey Trap (Honeybee Cozy Mystery)

The Buzz Kill (Honeybee Cozy Mystery)

Tea Shop Cozy Mysteries – Books 1-6

Hibiscus Homicide (Tea Shop Cozy Mystery)

Keeping Mums (Tea Shop Cozy Mystery)

Orange Juiced (Tea Shop Cozy Mystery)

Deathbed of Roses (Tea Shop Cozy Mystery)

Berry Murderous (Tea Shop Cozy Mystery)

Pushing Up Daisies (Tea Shop Cozy Mystery)

The Sweet Baked Mysteries - Books 1-6

Cinnamon and Sinfulness (Sweet Baked Mystery)

Raspberries and Retaliation (Sweet Baked Mystery)

Pumpkin Spice & Poisoning (Sweet Baked Mystery)

Blueberries and Bereavement (Sweet Baked Mystery)

Strawberries and Suffering (Sweet Baked Mystery)

Cupcakes and Conspiracies (Sweet Baked Mystery)

Food Bowl Mysteries Books 1-3

You're Kitten Me (Food Bowl Mystery)

Cat Red-Handed (Food Bowl Mystery)

An Impawsible Situation (Food Bowl Mystery)

The Only Secret Left to Keep (Detective Ngaire Blakes)

The Second Stage of Grief (Detective Ngaire Blakes)

The Three Deaths of Magdalene Lynton (Detective Ngaire Blakes)

Christchurch Crime Thriller Boxset

Breathe and Release (A Christchurch Crime Thriller)

Skeletal (A Christchurch Crime Thriller)

Found, Near Water (A Christchurch Crime Thriller)

ABOUT THE AUTHOR

Katherine Hayton is a middle-aged woman who works in insurance, doesn't have children or pets, can't drive, has lived in Christchurch her entire life, and currently resides a two-minute walk from where she was born.

For some reason, she's developed a rich fantasy life.

www.katherinehayton.com

Made in the USA
Lexington, KY
18 April 2019